Drama High, Vol. 5

LADY J

Drama High, Vol. 5
LADY J

L. Divine

KENSINGTON PUBLISHING CORP.
http://www.kensingtonbooks.com

DAFINA BOOKS are published by

Kensington Publishing Corp.
850 Third Avenue
New York, NY 10022

All Kensington titles, imprints and distributed lines are available at special quantity discounts for bulk purchases for sales promotion, premiums, fund-raising, educational or institutional use.

Special book excerpts or customized printings can also be created to fit specific needs. For details, write or phone the office of the Kensington Special Sales Manager: Kensington Publishing Corp., 850 Third Avenue, New York, NY 10022. Attn. Special Sales Department. Phone: 1-800-221-2647.

Dafina Books and the Dafina logo Reg. U.S. Pat. & TM Off.

ISBN-13: 978-0-7582-2534-4
ISBN-10: 0-7582-2534-2

First Kensington Trade Paperback Printing: April 2008
10 9 8 7 6 5 4 3

Printed in the United States of America

Acknowledgments

To Ivanna Brown, Vivian Bradberry, Kathy Shirley, Knieba Rodgers, Auntie Sonia, Auntie Paula, Taese, Karimah and Mbali: y'all make being queens look easy.

And, to my fans: always know your flow.

Prologue

After this morning's dream about my girl Mickey's man jumping Nigel, I never did get any sleep. Before our friends were awake, Rah made me breakfast and took me home to get dressed before taking me to work. He's such a sweetie. But the cuteness ended when he started to get repeat text messages and calls from his girl Trish, snapping me into the reality of the situation: if I want to be with Rah, I'll have to deal with being the other woman always, because I don't see him changing his ways anytime soon.

Thank goodness my mom's picking me up from work in a few minutes. I've never been so tired in my life, not even when Mama keeps me up all night working in the spirit room. I think it's my job that's wearing me down. I'm starting to feel like the people I see going to work on the bus everyday look miserable. I need to make a change for the better and soon.

"So how was your trip?" I ask as my mom pulls away from the curb and drives toward Inglewood. She decided to pick me up from work so she can get me back to Mama's early. I guess she and Karl have a follow-up to their Vegas date later this evening. Girls in general are a trip when they get a new man. And my mom's no exception to the rule.

"It was wonderful," she says, her green eyes sparkling through her Versace shades. They must be a gift from her new man because I know they're not in her budget. "But the date's not over yet. We're going to The Cheesecake Factory for dinner, so you've got ten minutes to get your stuff when we get back, okay? I'll wait for you downstairs."

Damn, it's like that? It seems second nature for women to put a guy as top priority when he's around. That's exactly why—no matter how much I may love Rah—I've decided not to have a man right now. Who needs the drama?

"I do, and so does every other woman I know, including you, little miss thang," my mom says telepathically. I hate when she does that.

"If you don't like it, then speak what's on your mind, shawty," she says again without moving her lips.

"Okay then, fine," I say, still vexed from having to work under Marty again today at the restaurant. I need to find a new job. "How come every time a new dude pops up I become second in line?" I say, feeling the pain of my words knot in my throat. Whenever I get emotional I want to cry. My mom sees it as a sign of weakness, so I try not to let it happen too often in front of her, and this time is no exception.

"You're never second, Jayd," my mom says. She's speeding down La Brea like it's the Autobahn. "But between working all week and having you on the weekends, I never have enough time to just be me," she says, sounding like the self-absorbed Lynn Marie that Mama always talks about. From the time I could remember, which has been basically all of my life, Mama has called my mother selfish and materialistic. I used to defend her, until I got a little older and understood that Mama was telling the truth; otherwise my mom would have raised me herself. I try not to blame her too much. Although it's times like these that make me rethink my forgiving attitude.

"Oh Jayd, I know you think I'm selfish, and you're right," she says, turning onto her street and unlocking the doors before stopping the car. "But honestly, Jayd, you've been able to take care of yourself since you were very young. When you get older you'll appreciate having such an independent mother. No matter how Mama may feel about it, I know you came to me because you knew who I was before we met. I used to talk to you in the womb all the time, and you responded. I know you heard me, so don't act like this is news," she says, touching my hand and looking at me. Except for their colors, our eyes are identical.

"I know, Mom, I know," I say, opening the car door and exiting before she makes me cry. I can actually remember having dreams about talking to my mother from inside her belly. Mama says it's typical for me and other babies born with cauls to have memories revealed through dreams, even of our past lives. Caught up in my thoughts, I trip on the curb, splashing the murky drain water onto my Nikes and accidentally causing the car door to scrape on the sidewalk.

"Okay then. So don't be so salty when I want to go out. It's all for you, baby. And be careful with that door," she says, forcing a sarcastic smirk from me. My mom's nothing if not honest about who she is and I definitely admire her for that. With or without a king-man, my mom's a queen. And I, being her daughter, wear a similar crown and deserve more than what any of these dudes around here are offering me. I know I can do better on my own and that's just what I intend to do.

~ 1 ~
Cruise Control

I don't mind being back on the bus and hiking the near-mile it takes to get to school every morning. Sometimes I wish Mama would let me attend school closer to home but she thinks I'll get into too much trouble. The brisk morning air feels refreshing against my cheeks. I can tell my legs have become a little weak from the daily rides with Jeremy. But I doubt I'll still receive that privilege now that we're no longer an item. I feel awful about our breakup. I do still have feelings for him, but they're not as strong as what I feel for Rah. Speaking of which, here's a text from him now. I'll have to hit Rah back later. Right now I want to mentally prepare for my day while hiking up this steep-ass hill—no distractions allowed.

As the procession of fancy cars passes me, all heading to South Bay High, I notice Misty walking ahead of me across the street. I guess her mom's running late this morning and couldn't give her a ride, since I saw her on each of the three bus rides it takes to get here. But luckily they were all packed as usual, forcing a safe distance between us.

I'm surprised Misty couldn't catch a ride with someone else from South Central. I guess she wanted to roll solo this morning, too. Still, it's odd for Misty to ride alone, unlike myself. I actually prefer the solitude I find on the bus; it gives me time to think. Mama says I should use this time to study my lessons, and I do for the most part. But instead of reading or writing them down, I recite what I already know in my head. It's hard enough to concentrate on these noisy and bumpy rides as it is. Besides, I don't like to have too much in my hands just in case I got to make a quick move. You never know when the driver will miss a stop or a fight will break out in the back. I'm always on my toes.

When I finally arrive on campus, Chance is waiting for me by my locker with Nellie and Mickey, of course. I must admit, I love having my crew back together. This weekend's chill session was just what we needed to get our groove back. And spending time with Rah is always cool, especially when we're in the studio watching he and Nigel work on their music. His new song still has me blushing, but not blind to the painful facts. Rah has a girl and I'm single. I've had three relationships in four months and it's time for me to chill. I'm letting time take over for now, leaving the controls on cruise while I sit back and enjoy the ride.

"Hey y'all," I say, interrupting what looks like a deep conversation. "What's up?"

"Hey Jayd," Nellie says, putting her lean arm around my shoulders and escorting me to my locker. What's her problem? "How are you feeling, girl?" she says as I open my locker door, retrieving my Spanish and English books for my first two classes. I haven't forgotten them in my locker for the past couple of weeks and I have to admit, I'm proud of my progress.

"I'm feeling fine, Nellie. Are you okay?" I say, putting my hand on her forehead, checking for a fever.

"Girl, stop playing," she says, slapping my hand away from her face and taking a step back toward Chance and Mickey, who are amused at our behavior. They look just as concerned about me as she does.

"Nellie's just making sure you're okay. This is the first day back since you and Jeremy broke up," Mickey says, taking her watermelon Blow Pop out of her mouth long enough to translate Nellie's body language. "Everyone's already talking about it."

"Yeah, it's pretty brutal," Chance says, grabbing Nellie by the waist, like she's his property to claim. Their blossoming relationship should be the talk of the town, not my breakup with Jeremy.

"Is there something I should know about you two?" I say, slamming my locker shut and leading the way out of the busy hall. I do notice people I don't even know looking at me and whispering to their friends. Bad news travels fast, especially when it's about the most wanted boy in school and his chocolate pick-of-the-month.

"Yeah, you should know that people are cashing in on their bets of how long you and Jeremy would last," Chance says, looking across the quad toward South Central, the black side of the quad, where Misty has joined the crowd. I'm sure she's having a field day with this one. I'm surprised she didn't say anything to me about it on the bus. But, from the looks of it, she had more important things on her mind. I'm still confused as to why KJ didn't give her a ride. Aren't they still dating?

"Yeah, it's pretty pathetic what some people will bet five dollars on," Mickey says. I can't say I'm surprised. Jeremy is the most popular cat at this wack-ass school and his life is of public interest.

"Only five dollars? I'm worth way more than that," I say, making light of the humiliating situation, while giving my friends a good laugh.

"Yes, you are," Chance says, letting go of Nellie long enough to give me a bear hug. "None of these dudes up here are good enough for my girl," he says, making Nellie feel slightly uncomfortable by the looks of it. Here we go. I don't like the idea of my best friends dating, especially not when Chance used to have a crush on me. Even though nothing went down between us, I know how females are when it comes to their men—even if they are my girls. Mickey would have had a beef with me if Nigel and I used to date. And I know it bothers Nellie that Chance used to have it bad for me. But now he's hooked on her, and I hope she concentrates on the future and not the past.

"Yeah girl, you already got your man," Mickey says, referring to Rah. "You just need to woman up and fight for the fool," she says, now loudly smacking her candy–turned–gum as the first bell rings.

"Nobody needs to woman up, Foxy Brown," I say, teasing my girl, who's still wearing the attitude of her Halloween costume's character. I'm glad we took pictures of that night at the Masquerade Ball—we all looked good. Noticing me eyeing my key chain before securing it into one of the many pockets on my Jansport, Nellie takes hers out and clasps it to her backpack.

"Hey, let's all wear our pictures on our bags, the ones of us in our Halloween costumes," she says, taking Chance's key chain off his belt and hooking it onto his backpack.

"What are we, in junior high?" Mickey says. Before she can protest any further, Nellie takes Mickey's out of her purse and locks it to her backpack as well.

"No. But we can still show love, right Jayd?" she says, waiting for me to follow suit. I take the picture off of my cluttered key chain and move it to my backpack, next to the "No More Drama" satchel Mama gave me for the first day of school. I

tied it there after the drama between Misty and Trecee un-
folded and haven't even considered moving it.

"Are you happy?" I say, sassing Nellie as we continue to
walk to class. "Now we officially look like the clique I never
wanted to be a part of."

"There's a big difference between our crew and those
other cliques," Nellie says, putting one arm around me and
the other around Mickey's shoulders, forcing Chance to release her waist again. Lucky for Nellie, Chance looks amused
by our impromptu soul train.

"What's that?" Mickey says, dryly. She's not into belonging
with any one set of folks, or any one dude for that matter. I
know she and her man have been together since junior high,
but I doubt that she's ever been exclusive. And, according to
the dream I had Saturday night, her unfaithful shit's about to
hit the fan.

"We're real friends—ride or die." As Nellie says something
that sounds more like Mickey's mantra, I see KJ and his crew
looking my way. He has a big smile on his face. I know he
must be talking about Jeremy and me breaking up. I wonder
if Jeremy's getting this kind of heat on the white side of
Drama High.

"Yeah, whatever," Mickey says. "Let's just try to stay on the
right side of our friendship from now on." I couldn't agree
more; we've already had enough drama for the year and
we're only in the second month of school. But I seriously
doubt it will happen. If I know one thing about our crew, it's
that we have haters. And where there are haters there's always drama. "And I haven't forgot about you being our slave,
either," Mickey says to Nellie, referring to Nellie's punishment for choosing Tania over us.

"I think she's learned her lesson, don't you?" I respond.
As much as I would love to humiliate Nellie for what she did,

no one's perfect, and I would hope my true friends would show me some mercy when the world's against me.

"No, especially not with her making us all wear these damned pictures on our backpacks," Mickey says, flicking the frame with her curved silver and violet nails. Nellie looks scared and I don't blame her. Knowing Mickey, Nellie's punishment will be cruel.

"There's the final bell," Chance says, pulling Nellie off to first period as I head to my Spanish class, saving my girl from her sentencing, for now.

"All right, I'll see y'all at lunch. I have to talk to my English teacher at break," I say. Mrs. Malone's helping me go over my last paper. She thinks I didn't try hard enough and wants me to revise it for an A. I wish all of my teachers were cool like her. Most of them would just let my little black ass fail.

"Damn, Jayd. School isn't all about work," Nellie says, as Chance leads her away.

"If I didn't know better, I'd say you loved this wicked-ass place," Mickey says, following the new couple away from the quad.

"Bye y'all. And don't make any more bets on my relationships," I yell after them. I know they didn't, but I'm sure the thought crossed their minds.

"Hey Jayd. What's up with my girl?" Nigel says, swooping me up into a huge hug and walking me out of my classroom as I head in. He loves catching me off guard. Nigel must've had a meeting with his coach, Mr. Donald, who also doubles as my Spanish teacher. Thank God I'm not trying to take the AP exam in this subject, because I'd fail because of his inadequate teaching, for sure.

"Nothing much. Aren't you going to be late for class?" I say, as he puts my feet back on the ground.

"I'm an athlete, baby," he says, showing off his hall pass from Mr. Donald. "We're always excused."

"Whatever, Nigel." I push the heavy door out of his hands and pass him. As I enter the classroom, I notice a new girl is sitting in my seat. She looks a little shaken, so I'm not going to sweat her today. I'll just have to be here a little early tomorrow morning to stake my claim.

"Have you talked to my boy this morning?" Nigel says, escorting me to an empty desk as the rest of the class makes their way into the chilly room. First period's always the coolest. I don't know if it's because of the morning frost, or the air conditioning they use to keep us awake, but I'm always glad to get out of this room.

"No, but he texted me a little while ago. I've just been too preoccupied to hit him back," I say, only telling half the truth. Ever since Rah's girl started texting him while we were together yesterday, I've been rethinking just how attached I want to get to him right now. I'm just glad he's not at my school everyday. If he were up in my face all of the time, he would be too irresistible for me to even think twice about getting back with him. Being tucked away at South Bay High does have its advantages.

"Well, you know he doesn't like to be kept waiting," Nigel says, grinning and showing off his bright smile. Mickey doesn't have a chance against falling hard for Nigel. I just have to help all of us not get hurt by the heat their forbidden love is stirring up. If Mickey's man finds out that she likes Nigel, there'll be hell to pay.

"Yeah, I remember well. And you will both remember that I don't play games," I say, taking my seat as Mr. Donald writes today's agenda on the board.

"Yeah, whatever, Jayd. You're a trip. Just hit him back," Nigel says, finally leaving the room, and me to my thoughts. I can't handle Rah and my first day broken up with Jeremy at the same time. I'm not looking forward to third period. I know Tania's got to be glowing over the news of us breaking up. I just hope she doesn't say anything to set me off, because the last thing I need is more heat in my fire this morning.

Second period was a breeze because we watched *The Color Purple* in class, comparing it to the novel, which we already read over the summer as a prerequisite for this course. I love Mrs. Malone's book list. She makes the best selections and also the most diverse. Our summer reading list included works from Sandra Cisneros, Zora Neale Hurston, and Julie Dash. I don't know if any of those authors will be on the AP exam for sure, but I enjoyed reading them anyway.

"Can I just rewrite my paper on Alice Walker's literary voice rather than Virginia Woolf's?" I ask, whining about my last assignment. I hated reading *A Room of One's Own*. Not because Woolf's writing sucks, but because I don't relate to her style. It just doesn't speak to me. And that's exactly what I tried to express in my paper.

"I like your critique of Ms. Woolf's voice," Mrs. Malone says after class, propping herself up onto the desk in front of mine, displaying her cream and turquoise moccasins. She looks like she just stepped out of a New Mexico tourist brochure. "You just need a more solid argument," she says, handing me a paper heavily marked in red. Damn, that means hella work on my end.

"It doesn't look like you liked much about it," I say, flipping each of the five pages, revealing more red ink as I continue to flip. It looks like she bled all over it.

"Jayd, all of these notes aren't bad. Don't always expect the worst," she says, leaning over and turning to the third page. "Take for example this page. I wrote a paragraph explaining how this is where your actual thesis begins, instead of on page one, which is where it belongs. This is your rough draft, Jayd. Turn in the final one to me by Friday," she says, closing the paper and placing it on the desk in front of me. "I've seen you do much better. But you've seemed a little distracted lately. Everything okay at home?"

"Yes, everything's fine," I say, looking at her wall clock, ready to roll. There are only five more minutes left in break and I really could use a Snickers right now. Mrs. Malone's always looking to have an after-school-special type of conversation with me. She's cool, but I'd never tell her all of my business. Mama would hang me where I stand if I ever told any of my teachers about my home life. I learned that lesson very early on when I was in elementary school: whether it's dirty or clean, we never air our laundry in public.

"Is everything okay with Jeremy?" she says, like we're a couple of old girlfriends having tea. Ah, hell nah, let me nip this one in the bud right now before she pulls out a box of tissues.

"Jeremy's no longer my concern," I say, rising from my seat, wounded report in hand. "I'll have the paper back to you by Friday and thank you again for giving me a chance to rewrite it." I say, marching toward the door. Damn, there's the first bell. Now I'm going to have to go to third period without my chocolate fix. I really hope everything's cool with both Jeremy and Tania. Any more irritation and I'm liable to bite someone's head off.

"Jayd, if you ever need to talk, I'm here. I know breaking up seems like the end of the world, but it's only high school," she says, whimsically dismissing my feelings as a schoolgirl crush. Even with Rah winning the battle for my heart, I still feel for Jeremy.

"Thank you, Mrs. Malone," I say, as I walk toward third period. Right now I just feel like my feelings are out of control, like they're marching to their own beat and I'm a passenger along for the ride.

*   *   *

"*The key is to be in alignment with your feelings in order to control the situation*," my mom says, sounding more like Mama than herself, as she invades my thoughts.

"Not at school," I say aloud to my mom as she coquettishly grins in my head. She's having too much fun with her born-again powers. But I know she's right. I have to get my mojo back, and fast.

When I walk into Mrs. Peterson's class, Tania and Jeremy aren't there yet. At least they won't be able to catch me off guard. Now I have a moment to prepare myself.

"Hey Jayd," Jeremy says, walking into our class right as the bell rings and taking the seat next to me, as usual. I guess some things haven't changed.

"Hey," I say, unable to muster up a different greeting. I'm still so upset with him for not claiming his and Tania's baby, because he's afraid of his dad disowning him, but I also feel guilty, because it was an easy way for me to be free to explore something new with Rah. But Jeremy doesn't have to know all that.

"Good morning, class," Mrs. Peterson says, barely looking up from her desk. "Your assignment's on the board. Your quiz will be during the last fifteen minutes of the period. If you must talk, make it quiet, please." Before returning to her newspaper, Mrs. Peterson looks up at the opening door, ready to attack whoever's walking into her arena late. "Thank you for joining us this morning," she says, hella salty to a tardy Tania.

"Well, it's the least I can do, considering it's my last morning at South Bay," Tania says, sliding an envelope across the teacher's desk, as giddy as ever. She turns around to wink at Jeremy, then gives me a sly look before walking to the back of the classroom where her followers are seated. She collects money from some classmates while Mrs. Peterson signs her release papers. I know this trick didn't place a bet on me and Jeremy.

"Jeremy," she says, leaning across my desk, directly in striking distance. If I were a crocodile, she'd be underwater by now. "It's been real," she says, blowing him a kiss as she cuts her eyes at me. "So sorry the two of you didn't work out," she says, showing off her fifty dollar bill and blinged-out engagement ring before walking back to the teacher's desk. The broad's lucky she's pregnant. Otherwise, whipping her ass might be worth the automatic suspension from school.

"What a bitch," Jeremy says under his breath, but loud enough to make the students around us giggle. Well, at least Jeremy and I are in agreement about something. Too bad I can't agree with Jeremy accepting that his father will only allow his sons to bring home white babies. Lucky for Tania, her parents hooked her up with a fiancé in New York who also happens to be rich. What a life.

"Yeah, I think our breakup is worth a whole lot more. At least a c-note," I say, breaking the iceberg that's between us. I would love it if we could still be friends. I genuinely like the cat, and love vibing with him, whether we can kiss or not.

"I agree. At least a hundred. I wish they'd let me in on the bet. I could have made a killing," he says, taking his books out of his backpack and turning to our assignment. With Tania's grand exit over, it's back to work in Government class.

"I hear you. What would you have wagered?" I ask, copying the notes from the board into my notebook. I miss the easy exchanges with Jeremy. We seemed to lose our spark amid all of the relationship baggage. It's nice to be on the path to friendship again, even if it's slightly awkward. Like Mama says, time heals all wounds or makes you forget what you were fighting about in the first place.

"A million dollars," he says, looking as serious as a heart attack and surprising me, much like Nigel did earlier. "I would've bet that much that we'd stay together, if the situation and timing were different." I now realize Jeremy feels as bad as I do about us breaking up. The difference between us is that he has no one to catch his rebound. My phone vibrates with another message from Rah, making me blush. Damn, this sucks. Now I really feel uncomfortable.

"Quiet please," Mrs. Peterson says, ending the heat for now. I hope Jeremy and I can really be friends, even if he does find out about me and Rah. But, for now, I just pray that we can all chill for a minute before crashing head on into each other.

~ 2 ~
Who Got Next?

"All the boys keep jocking, they chase me after school/
What you know 'bout me?"

—LIL' MAMA

I've been thinking about Jeremy's comment since third period, and Lord knows I didn't need any more distractions
to keep me from concentrating in my math class. I'm just
glad that's over and I can get a break at lunch. I wish I could
spend lunch alone or in Ms. Toni's office, but here comes
one of my girls. Now there's no way to duck for cover.

"Hey Jayd," Nellie says as I put my books into my locker.
"How's our champion academic?" she says, putting her arm
around my shoulder as I close my locker and walk with her
toward the main quad. I guess we're chilling in South Central today. Otherwise we'd be headed in the opposite direction.

"Don't try and butter me up, because you know I can't
save you from Mickey. Where's your boy toy?" I say, referring
to Chance. I hope she's not using him out of convenience.
But, just like with Mickey and Nigel, I'm going to try and stay
out of their relationship as much as I possibly can. What I do
on the side to influence the relationship is my own business
and usually for everyone's benefit. But, other than that, I
want no part of it.

"Chance is catching up with his boys. He said he'd meet
us in South Central when he's done. Nigel and Mickey are

already in the lunch line. Come on," Nellie says, rushing me through the packed hall and out of the double doors. The bright sun hits my face, forcing me to squint as we make our way through the lively crowd. It seems like everyone of the nearly two thousand students decided to stay on campus for lunch today. I wonder if Jeremy's one of them. I already miss hanging off campus with him and his crew on the regular. I'm also going to miss him paying my way.

"I'm really not in the mood for a crowd right now," I say. Nellie looks like a warrior queen as she charges through the medley of fair bodies in complete contrast to ours, focused on her goal. I wonder if she knows how powerful she really is, with or without her silly Homecoming crown.

"Jayd, cheer up. It's a nice day and Tania's last. Don't let these fools up here get you down." Completely dismissing my wishes, she leads me to the cafeteria where half the student body is gathered.

"That's not what you were saying a few weeks ago when that picture of you was going around," I say, reminding her of her desire to be an ostrich not too long ago. "I just want to hide right now, Nellie. You of all people should be able to understand that. And I'm not even that hungry."

"Jayd, you have no reason to hide. And don't get salty with me, trying to bring up the past and all." As we reach the lunch line, as usual Mickey and Nigel, the inseparable duo, are together and I notice KJ and Misty in line, too. I wonder who's paying? Noticing my gaze, KJ looks up from Misty's behind long enough to give me a sly smirk. I roll my eyes at him and his obnoxious attitude. What did I ever see in that punk?

"Hey y'all," Mickey says, with Nigel nodding a "what's up" from the side of her neck where he's resting his head. These two make me slightly envious of having a relationship where public displays of affection are a constant requirement. KJ was too clingy, while Jeremy, wasn't affectionate enough. But

Rah is right on point when it comes to making a girl feel wanted.

"Don't you two ever get tired of hanging all over each other? It's so uncouth," Nellie says, sounding more like a proper old white lady than my homegirl from the CPT.

"Never," Nigel says, turning Mickey's face toward his and giving her the biggest kiss I've witnessed in a long time.

"Okay, that's enough. Sorry I asked," Nellie says, eyeing today's menu. "Jayd, want to split a veggie sandwich?"

"Sure," I say. I can't resist Subway's veggies and cheese. It's the only thing they have that I like, except for their cookies. "No mayonnaise, and extra mustard on my side, por favor."

"English, please," Nellie says, sounding disgusted by my response. She's worse than Bush when it comes to hating on our Spanish-speaking homies. Maggie, my Latina homegirl who's also the queen of her crew, can't stand her, even if she did convince all of El Barrio to vote for our princess of color. But Nellie would never acknowledge the love and that's just fine with Maggie. She can't stand Nellie's bougie ass.

"Please," I say, as salty as her comment was before. "Why are you such a tight ass? You know what I mean."

"Yes, and you know how to speak English," Nellie says, turning around to order our food. "We are in America now. Speak the language if you want to stay." The Mexican lunch lady stops serving us and just stares at Nellie, ready to go off. If we were in Compton, I'm sure she would have given Nellie a mouthful of Spanish and then some. But we're in Redondo Beach, where the students have more power than the cafeteria staff. Instead, the lady cusses Nellie out with her eyes and I feel her one hundred percent.

"Nellie, sometimes you can be so rude," I say, snatching my soda and bag of chips from her and walking away toward the lunch benches. I swear I'm embarrassed to be with Nellie

and Mickey sometimes. It gets tiring being around igno-
rance, even if these are my girls.

"Why are you tripping now?" Nellie says, with Mickey and
Nigel following right behind her. "I was just joking," she says,
taking a seat on the bench next to me and unwrapping our
foot-long sub. "Besides, it's not like Spanish is your native
tongue."

"Well, neither is English," I say, thinking back to my lessons
about my great ancestor, Queen Califia. I'm not sure which
West African tongue she spoke when she arrived in California, but I know it didn't sound a damn thing like what was already being spoken here. "Nellie, that argument isn't valid
because none of us are originally from here. Besides, as much
as you claim to be well-read, you should know that." I miss
having intellectual debates with Jeremy. Arguing isn't as frus-
trating when I feel like I'm learning something while getting
my point across.

"What's got your panties all up in a bunch?" Nigel asks, sitting down on the bench across from us, right beside Mickey.
They both have a cheeseburger meal, making my and Nellie's
lunch look like rabbit's food. I look around me. It's kind of
nice to see everyone outside hanging out. Some students are
playing hacky sack or ballin', and others are just chilling and
enjoying not being in class.

"Yeah, it sounds like you've got a chip on your shoulder,
girl. I thought Rah was supposed to work that out for you,"
Mickey says, kissing Nigel's neck before taking a sip of her
drink. Nellie looks at them in disgust, but manages a smirk to
signal her agreement with their sentiment.

"You're so nasty," I say, reaching across and smacking her
in the arm. "Everyone isn't appeased by physical stimula-
tion." Some couples forget about their issues when they touch,
which is what Rah's hoping will happen with us. But he knows
I'm not that easy.

"Well, maybe you should join our camp. It works," Mickey says, giving her and Nigel a good chuckle. This is why I wanted to chill alone today. I'm just not in the mood. And I have to get to work on rewriting my English paper. As I plan my escape route in my head, Jeremy walks up with Chance, making me feel even more like getting away. What the hell is he doing in South Central anyway?

"What's up," Chance says, greeting Nigel and the rest of us.

"What's up," Jeremy says, following suit and greeting the group—but his eyes are focused on me. "How'd you do on our quiz?" he says, trying to make small talk. Before I can respond, Tania and her crew leave the cafeteria with a farewell committee of mass proportions behind them. I guess the Homecoming queen leaving the school is a pretty big deal in their world. It means that the runner-up actually gets to become queen for the rest of the year, so they perform some sort of ritual recrowning from the queen to the senior princess. But who cares? Besides the dance, there's nothing else for the queen to really do until next year.

"I'm glad the heffa's leaving," Mickey says, loud enough for Tania and her crew to hear. But, because Mickey's of no consequence to them, they choose to ignore her.

"That makes three of us," Jeremy says, still eyeing me. I wonder what he's thinking. He looks extra yummy today, wearing an olive green rip sun T-shirt with some faded cargo shorts and his classic Birkenstocks. His hair is pulled back in a bandana, showcasing his bright blue eyes and rugged bone structure. He should give up surfing and become a model, for real. Even as fine as Jeremy is, he still can't hold a candle to Rah's glow. It's like comparing Chris Brown to Nas. They both may come in nice packaging, but only one has everything I'm looking for in a dude.

"For real. We've got enough rich bitches taking up space

in here. Don't you agree, Jayd?" Mickey's got that right. Misty's all the broad I can take. Tania was way too extra, just like Trecee. Now with them both out of the picture, maybe I can concentrate more on myself instead of on how to stay away from crazy girls. I've wasted enough time this school year with these dudes and their high-drama bitches.

"Yes, I do," I say, taking a bite of my sandwich before following up with a mouthful of Doritos. The food goes so well together, unlike this scene. Everyone's paired up, except for me and Jeremy, but I don't think the pressure is as intense for him. I've had about all I can take for one day. I need space to breathe.

"I don't mind them being rich," Nellie says, picking at her food. "It's just the bitch part that bothers me." At least she's keeping it real. If Nellie had it her way, I know she'd be over there hanging with the rest of the royalty. I feel bad for my girl—her dream of winning the Homecoming crown came true, but ended up being a nightmare instead.

"I'm going to go to drama class early and study my lines," I say, clumsily rewrapping my sandwich and stuffing my chips in the bag alongside it. "The auditions for the Fall Festival are coming up next week and I'm trying out for Lady Macbeth," I say, knowing no one heard me. I pick up my soda and backpack, ready to walk down the hill when Tania heads my way. Shit, sometimes I'm too slow with my escapes. I need a refresher marathon of *The Bourne Identity* if I'm going to escape trouble at this school.

"Already missing me, Jeremy?" Tania says, wrapping her arms around his neck and kissing him on the cheek, while everyone watches, waiting for my response. Reid and Laura, the president and first lady of the Associated Student Body or ASB as we call it, are even on the sidelines watching the show.

"No, Tania, I'm not," he says, taking her hands in his and forcing her off of him. How can he be so cold to his baby-mama, even if they aren't claiming each other? Dudes are a trip.

"Not even a little bit?" Tania says, backing off, but still flirting with her eyes. A rich slut is the worst kind. I bet she'd fit right in with Paris Hilton and her crew. Maybe she'll run into them while she's in the Big Apple.

"Could y'all take your soap opera somewhere else? We're trying to eat over here," Mickey says, again catching Tania's eye. I don't even know what made Tania think she could come over to where Mickey was sitting and feel safe, especially after what went down at the Halloween dance a few days ago. I thought Mickey was going to kill Tania for attempting to plant a worm-infested apple in the cauldron for Nellie to bite into. Too bad Laura took the bait instead.

"No one's talking to you. And besides, it's a free country last I checked," Tania snaps back. Now she's done it. Mickey puts the remainder of her burger in its container and wipes her hands and mouth on a napkin before slowly rising from her spot next to Nigel, who's smiling because he knows what's about to go down. Nothing's more amusing to guys than a chick fight.

"I don't care if the bitch is pregnant," Mickey says, looking at Jeremy, but talking to no one in particular. "She's about to get her ass whipped once and for all, talking to me like she knows me. Your last day here's going to be the most memorable day of your life," Mickey says, tossing her drink at Tania, who unwillingly catches it as red fruit punch splashes across her pink sundress, highlighting her flat chest. I hope the baby gives her some breasts.

"You—you—hoochie!" Tania shouts, as the crowd around our table gets bigger. I wish I could leave and head to class like nothing's happening. But Mickey's my girl and she wouldn't hate Tania so much if it weren't for Nellie and me. So, the least I can do is have her back. Noticing my discomfort, Chance comes over to me and stands by my side, with Nellie right behind him. It's nice to see him taking some initiative for a change.

"Is that right?" Mickey says, walking around the lunch bench, ready to charge. "Hoochie is as hoochie does, trick!" She lunges at Tania, grabbing her hair as Jeremy blocks her full attack.

"All right, break it up," Jeremy says. Nigel pulls Mickey back as we watch the hectic scene in astonishment. I don't think anyone even heard the bell ring. The cafeteria locking up is my only indicator that it's time for us to go. I hope this is the last time I see Tania—forever.

"This is what you chose over me and our crew," Tania says to Jeremy as he lets her go. For the first time, I can sense her pain. So, she's not completely heartless? Good to know. "You'd rather hang out with a bunch of rough ghetto girls than me?" And, just like that, I change my mind. This broad is as cold as they come. I feel sorry for their baby.

"Who are you calling ghetto?" Nellie yells at her. I know she wants to kick her ass for the whole rotten apple incident, but that'll never happen. Nellie's way too prissy to fight. That's why she's got Mickey.

"You and your raggedy little friends. This school used to stand for something. But now anyone can come here as long as they have a bus pass. I'm glad I'm leaving this tired scene." As she walks toward Laura, who's dutifully waiting with a handful of napkins, I feel like I have to say something. This is, after all, really my fight.

"I'd rather be ghetto any day, than give up my life in high school to take the GED so I can become one of the *Desperate Housewives*." I say, causing oohs and ahhs to ripple through the crowd. Patting herself dry, Tania looks genuinely pierced by my sharp remark. I know being pregnant and single wasn't part of her ten-year plan, no matter how she tries to play it off.

"I may be a housewife, but I'm never desperate," Tania says confidently. But I can tell she's shaken. Between my mouth and Mickey's physical attack, I'm surprised the girl's still standing.

"Are you sure about that?" I say, ready to let everyone know exactly why she and Jeremy broke up. Luckily, Rah texts me right in time, silencing my exposé. Besides, I don't want to be late for class. I can channel all of my frustration toward my rehearsal. Lady Macbeth is a raw chick and I'm going to need to release this anger somewhere. So, Shakespeare will have to do.

"For real, ladies, just chill out," Jeremy says. I look at his face, knowing he's afraid I'll spill the beans. But I'm not; I'm done with their mess. I have my own life to live and they're not included.

"I hope you live happily ever after, Cinderella," I say, as Chance, Nigel, my girls and I all head away from the scene. Mickey devours the last of her lunch while the crowd rushes toward fifth period. I guess she worked up an appetite wailing on Tania. I'm still a little hungry myself. I can't wait to go home. Only two more classes until I'm free from this madness. Why can't I ever have a peaceful week at this school?

When I arrive on my block after school, the scent of dinner is overwhelming. I love walking down our street in the evening. I don't see how my uncle Bryan can be a full-on vegetarian, especially living with Mama. It's cool to go "no meat" for lunch every once in a while, but Mama's got me sprung on southern cooking—no tofu included.

"Your grandparents are at it again," my neighbor Brandy says from her porch. It smells like fried chicken's cooking in her house. My cousin Jay comes out right behind her like he lives there. He and my uncles all have their homes-away-from-home around the neighborhood.

"Yeah Jayd. You might want to sit this one out," Jay says, devouring a chicken sandwich as my stomach growls.

"I can't. I'm too hungry." The veggies and cheese sub didn't do me justice and I'm ready to grub. I hope Mama cooked because I could use a home-cooked meal after the day I've had.

"Well, you'd better order a pizza because the kitchen's a wreck," Jay says, putting the last of his dinner into his mouth.

"What happened to the kitchen?" I ask. I hope the damage isn't too bad. I could at least warm up some fishsticks or make a peanut butter and honey sandwich or something.

"Mama's wrath, that's what," he says, laughing and taking a seat on the porch steps. "She went way the hell off on Daddy and his latest admirer. You should've been there earlier when the chick was still there. Mama made her cry just by looking at her."

"Your grandmother's green eyes are powerful. Are those contacts? Because if they are, I need me some of them," Brandy says, loudly smacking her gum. If she only knew how powerful Mama really is she'd never joke about Mama's sight. She and everyone else around here know that Mama's eyes are real, and so are her powers.

"They didn't have to call the police, did they?" I ask. The Compton Police probably have our phone number on speed dial, with all of the shit that goes down at our house.

"No, but it was pretty brutal," Brandy says, taking a seat next to Jay while I post up against her fence. "But I ain't mad at your grandmother. That woman was wrong for coming up in her house like that and bringing your granddaddy dinner, like he doesn't have a wife."

"Was it the same woman who brought that pound cake

last time?" I say, remembering Daddy picking up the broken pieces of the dessert from the ground. Mama doesn't play when it comes to defending her territory, which begins and ends at home.

"Yes, it was," Jay says. He loves to gossip more than any woman I know. I think most men secretly do. "She knew what she was doing. But I don't think she knew what she was getting herself into," he says, laughing at the memory.

"I wish some chick would come up to my man's house bringing him food like he's single. I'd beat her ass right where she stood," Brandy says, rising from the bottom porch step, displaying her six-month-pregnant belly. Brandy's in the same class as Jay and her older sister Kendra, who also attends Compton High and already has a one-year-old son.

"Yeah, that was kind of bold. But Daddy puts it on them from the pulpit, I guess," Jay says. That sandwich didn't come from Brandy's kitchen. I wonder who made a chicken run. It could have been Bryan, but he wouldn't go to a chicken spot as a first choice because he doesn't eat meat, which means he probably didn't make this run. And none of my other uncles are driving right now.

"I think it's what he's putting on them away from the pulpit that's got your grandmother pissed," Brandy says, stepping into the house as Jay gets up to run after her. I know he wishes that baby in her belly was his. But she only goes for gangstas: the rougher the better. Her man, Bull, is constantly in and out of jail and scares the shit out of me when he's around. I don't see why she got pregnant by him in the first place. But to each her own, I guess. It doesn't help that her mother left Brandy and Kendra in this house alone with their little brother, who's my age and is now in juvenile hall for stealing car radios with his fellow gang members, one of whom just happens to be Brandy's baby-daddy, who didn't get caught this time.

"I'll catch y'all later," I yell after them as I continue my stroll toward home. I've learned to deal with all of the fighting in our home over the years. Not that I've grown immune to it, but I know where to hide if need be. But getting dinner out of a destroyed kitchen is another challenge entirely.

When I reach home, I see Mama's dog, Lexi, sitting on the front porch, guarding the fortress. I also notice Daddy sitting across from Mama at the dining room table. Neither one of them notices me gazing through the window, so I know they're in serious discussion mode. Rather than disturb them, I think I'll go and chill in the spirit room. Maybe I can bake some biscuits or something while I'm out there.

As I make my way through the weathered wooden gate leading to the backyard, I notice a cloud of smoke coming from the closed garage. I bet my uncles are getting high and trying to ignore the show going on inside.

"What are y'all doing in here?" I say, entering the stuffy space. The television blares loudly from the corner, allowing some light into the otherwise dark room. I make out three bodies. One is definitely Bryan, the other I'm guessing is Bryan's best friend Tarek, and the other is a little hazy. I know it's not another one of my uncles, who I'm sure are all out causing trouble of their own.

"What's up, Jayd?" Rah's voice bellows through the cloudy haze. A person can get high just from smelling this shit.

"Raheem, what are you doing here? And where's your car?" I say as I make my way over to where he's seated behind the folding card table in the center of the floor.

"Up the street at Rodney's house. He's putting in a new stereo for me. You would have known that if you'd bother to return a nigga's messages," he says, sounding irritated with me.

"I was just about to call you. But now I don't have to," I say, sitting in his lap and putting a smile on his face. "I really could use a hug without all of the heat, please." Sensing how tired I am, Rah passes up his turn in the rotation and puts his arms around me, making all of my troubles melt away. Too bad the fix is only temporary.

"Bad day?" he asks as he takes my backpack from my lap and places it on the floor next to us. My uncle looks completely faded and although Tarek doesn't smoke, he looks as chill as the rest of them.

"Yes, but it's much better now." His scent of Egyptian Musk oil mixed with Unforgivable—my favorite cologne— calms me down, almost making me forget about my hunger. But my stomach hasn't forgotten and now everyone in the room knows it.

"You hungry? We've got some Popeye's," Rah says, pointing to the stacked table. This impromptu session is just what I needed to chill me out. I grab a bag with a two-piece meal in it. This will definitely hit the spot. If Rah were any other friend, I wouldn't be too cool with him popping up at my house, especially not with Mama and Daddy at each other's throats. There's just something about Rah that feels comfortable, like he already belongs here. But when the wrong friends get too close, it's anything but comfortable.

~ 3 ~
Too Close For Comfort

"Don't forget where you are and where you've been/
Life's lessons then made you into woman."

—GLENN LEWIS

After Rah left last night, I stayed behind in the spirit room until midnight working on my English paper and studying my spirit work. I found a recipe to help clear up all of the negative energy around us. I'm not the only one dealing with cheating dudes and trifling female trouble; so are my mom and Mama. That's why last night's lesson from my great-grandmother Maman was so important. It was about how everything we do affects our lineage, as well as others around us. That's why our heads always have to be in a state of calm so that we can make the best decisions and, most of all, wield our powers carefully.

Mama was at the shrine all night long, praying and crying. Whatever's going down between her and Daddy must be big. She finally went to sleep right before I came in and I was glad. Mama needs her rest and all of this commotion isn't good for her nerves. I'll make sure to put her herbs and water by the bed this morning before I leave. She needs to keep herself up in order to deal with all of our haters. I also grated some fresh coconut and cocoa butter and wrapped them in cotton gauze before sprinkling lavender and eucalyptus oil on the combination and placed it in her eye pack before resting it on her face last night. According to the spirit book, the ingredients will help her to see clearly and cool her head. She hasn't slept with it on lately, but I hope it will help her to get some much needed rest.

"Jayd, are you up?" Bryan whispers through the closed bedroom door. It's almost five-thirty in the morning and if I stay in bed any longer I risk missing the first bus. I wish I didn't have to get up so early. It seems so unfair that Jay gets to sleep in an entire hour later than I do because he can walk to school from here.

"Yeah, I'm up," I grunt as I smack my alarm clock before it goes off. Mama must be in a deep sleep because she hasn't moved a muscle since last night and she's usually more dependable than the Tasmanian Devil's ringing every morning. I guess the eye sack I made is working after all.

Making my way out of my bed and to the back of the door where my clothes are hanging, I open it to find Bryan clearing out of the bathroom. He's more polite than my other uncles. They usually leave shit everywhere, which is why I try to get in and out before they do.

"Here you go, little queen," he says, checking his reflection in the mirror one more time before stepping out of the steamy room. "It's pure, now you may enter."

"Whatever, fool," I say, as he smacks me with his towel, which I grab and tug out of his hand.

"Give it back," he says, reaching for it as I attempt to close the bathroom door and get some privacy.

"You need to learn to keep your hands to yourself," I say, as we struggle for the towel. Finally giving up, I let go and Bryan falls to the floor, almost loud enough to wake up the household. But, after yesterday's excitement, I guess everyone's worn out.

"I let you win," he says, gathering his fallen toiletries from the floor around him and rising to his feet.

"This wasn't tug of war, fool. That's what's wrong with dudes; y'all always playing games, even when there's no opponent."

"Like I've told you before, Jayd," Bryan says, leaning up against the hallway wall, "girls play games, too. But for real, though." He displays his charming smile. He's got so many girls it should be a crime—I'm sure it is in some countries. "Can I borrow five dollars? I get paid tomorrow. I'm good for it."

"Five dollars?" I say, closing the bathroom door in his face. "You're my uncle. I should be asking you for a loan."

"Come on, Jayd. It's hard out here for a pimp," he says through the door. Running my water, I hang my clothes up and realize I left my toiletries in my bag in Daddy's room. It's already bad enough that we all have to share rooms, but there's not enough closet or drawer space for me to keep all of my things in one place. I'll be glad when the day comes that I can get rid of the three large Hefty trash bags that hold my stuff in Daddy's closet, which is also where Jay and Bryan keep their clothes. Daddy uses the larger closet next to his bed across from the bunk beds where Bryan and Jay sleep. What I'd give to have my own room, let alone my own bathroom.

"Then stop pimpin'," I say, opening the door and stepping into his room ahead of him. Daddy and Jay are still asleep and the closet door is already open, allowing me quick access.

"So you're not going to help a brotha out?" Bryan says, sounding like a wounded puppy. Why is he always broke?

"You better give it back to me first thing tomorrow," I say, reaching into my small purse and handing him a five dollar bill. I keep my purse with me everywhere in this house. Things have a tendency to walk away from me if I'm not careful.

"I got you and then some," he says, taking the money and heading back into his room to finish dressing, leaving me to start my day. The official plan is to hide out in the library all day and get as much work done as I can—no drama allowed.

The last bus ride is nice and calm this morning, unlike the first two. It seemed like everyone wanted to be early today. I had to stand the entire trip for both rides. Dudes don't even give up their seat for the elderly, let alone a girl these days. I guess chivalry really is dead. I must admit, I already miss my daily rides from Jeremy. But, I'm ready to get my own ride. Until then, I'm at the mercy of city transportation. I wish the bus dropped me off a little closer to campus but I'll take what I can get.

As if he heard my wish, Jeremy turns onto Prospect Avenue headed to school but I don't expect him to give me a ride. After all, I did break up with him and he doesn't owe me anything. But to my surprise he notices me and looks almost happy to see me.

"Would the lady care for a ride?" Jeremy says, pulling alongside me before I begin my hike up the steep hill.

"Are you sure? Isn't that a boyfriend type of duty?" I say. Truthfully, I could use the lift this morning. I'm exhausted from staying up late and my legs aren't used to the walk anymore.

"Friends get rides too, Lady J," Jeremy says as he reaches across the passenger seat and opens the heavy door. As Daddy would say, they don't make cars like these anymore. Classic Mustangs like this one are hard to come by, and so are gentlemanly men. "We're friends, right?" he says, looking up at me from under his cap brim. His eyes, like Mama's, are irresistible.

"Fine," I say as I fall into the cream-colored leather seat. This five-minute ride is saving me fifteen minutes of a good workout and I'm grateful. But he doesn't need to know that. The last thing I want is for him to feel like I need him. That'll go to his head and the next thing I know he'll be trying to get back with me again, I'm sure.

"Well, don't be overjoyed," he says, pulling away from the curb toward campus. It's foggy, so there's no view of the ocean. "I'm glad to see you this morning."

"Oh really? And why is that?" I ask, allowing the lyrics of the alternative music on the radio to pull me in, rather than play his mind games. I don't know who it is, but it sounds cool.

"Well, I wanted to say I'm proud of you." Is he serious? What could he be proud of me for?

"What are you talking about?" I say. Mickey pulls up beside us in her pink Regal bumping Snoop. Nellie, sitting in the passenger seat, notices us together and smiles big.

"Good morning, you two," Nellie says. I know I'm going to get it for this.

"What's up, ladies?" Jeremy says, honking at Chance, who's parked across from the spot Jeremy's pulling into. I also see Matt and Seth across the way. I have to time my audition for the play with the bus schedule, and they're the men in charge of getting me in and out on time. I also want to practice my lines with someone auditioning to play the lead role of *Macbeth,* and I'm sure they'll have that information too.

"So, do I hear reconciliation in the works?" Nellie chimes. Mickey's unamused, and I have a feeling I'm going to get a mouthful from her and Nigel before the day's over. Now I really have a good reason to hide out.

"It's just a ride, y'all," I say, opening the car door and stepping out before Jeremy even turns off the engine.

"Whatever. I've got to find somewhere to park. I'll holla at you later," Mickey says, pulling off. I can tell by her tone she's pissed. I can't deal with that right now. I want to get back to why this dude is proud of me, like he's my daddy. I've got to hear this one.

"So, as you were saying about your pride in me," I say, leaning up against his trunk, watching his lean body as he pulls himself out of the low vehicle. I love tall men.

"I'm proud you didn't sink to Tania's level. She can get real dirty." Now see, that's what irritates me about Jeremy. He can be so judgmental sometimes, even if he doesn't mean to be. It's all in his tone.

"How can you think so badly about a girl you made a baby with?" I say. How is it that dudes get amnesia about a girl's personality when they sleep with her, but have a perfect recollection of what a bitch she is after it's all over? If this is how sex affects the brain, I might stay a virgin forever.

"What's your problem? I'm just calling it like I see it," he says, locking his car and leading the way to the main campus.

"You shouldn't talk bad about Tania, even if I do agree with you. She's carrying your seed," I say, sounding like Rah. I remember getting this speech when he got my homegirl pregnant a few years back. He was right, and the same principle holds true in this situation. He slept with her. Now he has to pay the price, even if he doesn't like her. KJ went through the same thing with his ex-chick Trecee but got lucky because Shae revealed Trecee was already pregnant before KJ started messing with her. I hope he doesn't repeat the same mistake with Misty. She may be a trick but she's no slut, so I'll know the baby's his.

"Whatever, Jayd. Look," he says, stopping in front of me and causing the other students walking around us to stop and stare. "I made a mistake getting Tania pregnant, but it's over now. Can we just move on?"

"Over? How the hell is it over when she's still in her first trimester?" I say, almost shouting. Jeremy shoots me a look that tells me to keep my voice down. And he's right: this conversation's over. The first bell's about to ring and I don't want to be late for my day of hiding. I also have AP meetings tomorrow to prepare for and I don't want to give Mrs. Bennett anything else to complain about, so I better check my English portfolio to make sure it's on point. "I have to go. Excuse me," I say, walking around him and joining the crowd.

"Jayd, come on," Jeremy says, catching up to my brisk pace. But I'm done talking. It's getting us nowhere and I've already made my decision. Whether he accepts it or not is up to him. "Don't be like this."

"Don't be like what, Jeremy? Compassionate? God forbid I'd want to do that. Oh, that's right. You don't believe in God," I say as I turn toward him and shoot a look that silences him once and for all. I turn back around on my heels and march toward my locker. I hope Mickey and Nellie aren't there because I'm really not in the mood to be grilled right now. I need to calm down and focus on all of the work I have ahead of me. I don't have time for anyone else's bull today.

My locker would be jammed this morning. By the time I get it open I only have enough time to get my books and get to class. Before I exit the main hall, I see KJ, C Money, and Del leaving the main office. I still don't understand why Misty couldn't catch a ride with them to school. But why do I care? I have enough on my mind as it is.

"You can't speak, girl?" KJ shouts down the corridor. He and his boys all look alike, with their Adidas warm-up suits and the shoes to match. They're a good-looking crew. Too bad they're all jackasses.

"I'm speaking," I say as I roll my eyes and exit the hall, only to find my girls outside waiting for me. Damn, to be the second largest school in Southern California, South Bay seems too small sometimes.

"Hey girl," Nellie says, falling into step with me as Mickey trails behind. I can feel her eyes burning through the back of my skull. Let me set them straight right now so we don't have any issues.

"Before y'all say anything, Jeremy saw me at the bus stop, offered me a ride, I accepted, we argued, nothing more. Any questions?" I say as we make our way through the oncoming traffic of students rushing to classes.

"Yeah," Mickey says, now in sync with us. "Why did you get in his car in the first place?" I sometimes hate that she's formed an alliance with Nigel and Rah, because now she's going to be looking out for my boys and not me, which is not the way it should be since she's supposed to be my homegirl. As many times as Rah's been in the wrong, Nigel's never ratted him out to me. But I think Mickey would love to bust my chops right in front of them both and that ain't cool.

"Because my legs were tired. But, you wouldn't know anything about that since your man makes sure you always have a ride, and a car when you can drive," I say, a little more sour than necessary. But she's really got her nerve this time.

"Put the claws away, ladies," Nellie says, a little too jovial for the moment. "We can continue this lively discussion at break."

"I can't. I have too much work to do," I say, heading to my Spanish class and leaving them to go their separate ways. At least we don't have any classes together. I couldn't concentrate on my schoolwork if I had them up in my grill on a daily basis.

"Well then, we'll catch up after school at Nigel's practice. Since it's an early day, Mickey can give you a ride home, isn't that right, girl?" Nellie says, but that doesn't look like what Mickey was thinking at all. How can Mickey seriously hate on me when she's juggling two dudes herself? What the hell is up with the hypocrites this morning? When it's too close to home, the truth can get mighty uncomfortable.

"Yeah, whatever," Mickey says, folding her arms across her chest and revealing her freshly airbrushed nails, gold hoop charms and all. Must be nice to have a dude's bankroll to count on.

"Okay, it's settled. We're hanging after school, no excuses," Nellie chimes, again trying to lighten the mood, but I'm not feelin' it.

"Fine. I've got to go," I say. The last thing I want to do is sit up at Nigel's practice after school when I could use the time to study or nap or do something more productive than talk about Rah and Jeremy. Honestly, neither of them can give me what I want or need right now, so the topic is moot. But I know my girls don't see it that way, and I'm sure even Chance and Nigel will add their two cents if they have the opportunity.

Now that Rah has allies who were my friends first, I feel like Rah attends our school. Now, let Rah do some shady shit and we'll see how far the loyalty of our so-called friends-in-common extends. His ears must be burning because here he is, texting me good morning. If I didn't love this boy so much, I wonder if we'd still be friends.

The afternoon sun has melted away the fog and is shining brightly, giving me plenty of much needed warmth. My attitude always improves when the weather's good. And I needed the adjustment, especially to deal with my girls giving me heat about Jeremy. I know they mean well, but really. Enough is enough. I didn't even speak to him in third period, although he tried to pass me notes during our boring movie. But I've had enough of him for one day.

* * *

"You need to let that white boy know that y'all can't be friends anymore. That's what you need to do," Mickey says, sipping on her grape Crush while Nigel and the other football players work it out on the field. We're sitting in the middle of the bleachers where the sun is shining its brightest and providing us with some much needed warmth on this cool afternoon. The day went by fast because of the teacher's meetings being held today, which gives us an extra hour and a half of kick-it time. I have to make it a point to holla at Ms. Toni tomorrow. It seems like forever since we caught up and I know she's already gotten wind of my breakup with Jeremy.

"Now, why can't they be friends?" Nellie says, looking around for Chance. I know she'd never admit it, but the girl is sprung and I can see how. Chance has always had her back and has liked her even longer. All it took was for Nellie to come around and now they can love without limit. "So, he's made a few mistakes. That's what friends do, they mess up and they forgive," she says, reflecting more on our friendship than on Jeremy and me.

"Yes, but they aren't homies. Like I said before, dudes can't be friends with girls. It ain't natural. Especially not after y'all have made out," Mickey says, smiling as I remember when Jeremy first kissed me at the beach. Yeah, that wasn't a very friendly interaction at all.

"Yeah, even kissing can be deadly to a friendship," I say, still strolling down memory lane. I remember my first kiss with Rah. After that, I was sprung. Same thing happened with this dude named Donovan. I was his first kiss and we never went back to being friends. And now Jeremy.

"What are you talking about? Nigel and Jayd are just friends, Chance and Jayd are just friends and I'm sure there are better examples, too," Nellie says, sounding as optimistic as ever. But I'm siding with Mickey on this one, even if I hate to admit it.

"I think you're right, Mickey, but not because I don't think Jeremy and I can just be friends," I say, snacking on my left-over chips from lunch. "I don't think I can ever get over the way he gave up the rights to his baby, especially when he thinks Tania is Satan's love child. How could he allow his baby to be raised by her without at least knowing who her husband-to-be is?"

"Yeah, that is messed up," Nellie says. And I know she feels me. Her daddy is actually her stepfather. But he's also the only father she's ever known and that must bother her a little.

"I hate to burst your bubble, but I'm just being real. I can't have any respect for the way he's treating Tania, and without respect there's no true friendship, is there?" I say as I send Rah a quick text before he sends out an APB. We got that straight last night: always respond to each other's messages in a timely manner.

"You've got that right. I'm just glad you see it my way," Mickey says, stabbing Nellie's ego with her words. So, how's Rah?" she says, reading my mind.

"He's cool. He caught up with me yesterday after school," I say, leaving out the details of my dramatic evening. I hope today is much less eventful when I get home.

"Now see, that's a real friend for your ass," Mickey says, finishing the last of her soda before moving on to her pork rinds. She must've brought those with her because I know they don't sell them up here. Just then, we hear a car with heavy bass coming down the street parallel to the football field. Pulling into the parking slots at the top of the stadium, we see Mickey's man getting out of his black Monte Carlo and heading our way. Oh shit, this can't be good.

"What the hell is he doing here?" Nellie says, alarmed at the possibility of another fight, and I feel her. The last thing I want to do is get involved with Mickey's man and their arguing, especially not with Nigel here. That's more than I can handle today.

"Mickey," her man shouts from the top of the bleachers. In navy blue Dickies and a white wife-beater, he looks like a straight thug. Half of his hair braided and the other half is in a ponytail, and he looks pissed. "Get up here, now."

"Why you gotta yell at me like that?" Mickey says, simultaneously talking shit and gathering her stuff up. She knows better than to give him too much lip in public.

"Because you're obviously deaf since you didn't hear your phone ringing. I've been calling and texting you for the past hour. I know you got out early," he says as she meets him halfway up the stairs. I look toward the field to see Nigel staring up at us, ready to charge like a bull seeing red. Luckily the coach has them running drills, so he can't leave the field right now unless he wants to miss playing in Friday's game. But if something goes down between Mickey and her man, I know he'll be up there in a flash, game or no game.

"I'm sorry, baby. I've been talking to my girls," she says, only telling half the truth. Before she sat down with us, she and Nigel went to the car to kick it. I'm sure she turned her phone off then and forgot all about it, putting her man's jealousy radar on red alert.

"You were supposed to finish braiding my hair today," he says. Man, she's got him in check. How does she do it?

"Oh, my bad. I got you when I get home, boo," Mickey says, gently touching his half-done do. I really need to get my notebook out and take notes on this girl's pimping abilities, even if the pimping goes both ways in their relationship.

"And when will that be?" he says, grabbing her around the waist and staking his claim for all to see, including Nigel, who's just tripped in midair over nothing, falling to the ground. "The football players up here suck. Y'all need to come to Compton. That's where all the real niggas play."

"They don't all suck," Mickey says, instinctively defending her other man. "I'll be home right after I drop Jayd and Nellie off, okay baby?"

"No, now. I want you to finish braiding me outside before my curfew's up in a couple of hours. I got some business to take care of and I need to be on the porch to handle it," he says, glancing our way, which lets me know it's the same type of business that probably got his electronic ankle bracelet put on in the first place. "I'm sure your girls can find another way home."

"Okay, baby. I'm right behind you," Mickey says as he heads back to his car, embarrassed at how much control her man actually has over her. Not me. I'll never be at a dude's beck and call like this girl is. I don't know which fear for her is worse: that he'll cut her allowance off or that he'll whip her ass. Either way, my girl's getting played and she's allowing the game to continue.

"And how are we supposed to get home?" Nellie says, pissed to high heaven. Lucky for her Chance is coming our way. I'm sure he'll be glad to give her a ride when she's ready to go. If I leave now I can still catch my regular buses and leave all of this drama behind.

"And on that note, I'm out," I say, grabbing my backpack and heading back up to where Mickey's man is parked. I knew I should've stayed to myself all day long instead of kicking it down here.

"Jayd, wait," Nellie says, grabbing my arm as Mickey looks from me to her. She knows her man's patience is gone and she's taking too long to get back to him. He'll probably give her a ride to her car just to make sure she leaves right away. There's a thin line between chivalry and possessiveness and her man crossed it a long time ago.

"Hey ladies," Chance says, finally making it up the steep bleachers and immediately sensing the tension.

Before we can answer, Mickey rudely interjects, "Can you take them home?"

Chance looks at each of us and stops short of questioning when he sees Mickey's man waiting for her. He doesn't know who he his, but Chance senses he's part of our problem.

"I don't need a ride. I'm good," I say, removing my arm from Nellie's light grasp and continuing my trek. A Williams woman always has an exit plan.

"Are you sure?" Chance says. Even though I know he would give me a ride, he also wants to be alone with his new girl and I want to be alone—period.

"Very," I say. I just want to go home, eat something good and get some work done. I've had more than enough social interaction for the week and it's only Tuesday. Luckily, I have AP meetings at both of my breaks tomorrow and I'll be practicing for my audition in my free time on Thursday. At least the next couple of days will be slightly more peaceful, I hope.

~ 4 ~
Esmeralda

*"I'm the type of girl that'll look you dead in the eye/
I'm real as they come if you don't know why I'm fly-y-y-y-y."*

—TIMBALAND FT. NELLY FURTADO AND JUSTIN TIMBERLAKE

After my long week, going to my mom's this afternoon will be such a relief. Between my meetings and friends, I haven't had much time to myself. I think every relationship needs a break, including the ones that I have with my girls. Sometimes their issues are too much for me to handle, along with my own madness. I need a break from school in general, and Thanksgiving is in a few weeks. That'll be a good time to recuperate from this place, even if it's only a couple of extra days off.

Before I head out the back door to get to the bus stop, I notice Bryan coming in from his night job at the radio station. He's a very talented DJ and I admire him for keeping his volunteer gig, even if it means he has to work straight through the next day at Miracle Market. Speaking of which, he got paid yesterday, so he should have my money.

"What's up, Jayd?" he mumbles, grabbing the cornflakes from the top of the refrigerator and eating straight from the box, dropping crumbs onto the floor. I know he's tired, but other people live here too.

"You have no respect," I say, snatching the cereal from him and putting it on the table. "Get a bowl."

"Ok, lil mama," he says. I know I sound just like her, but

she's right. This house would be a pigsty if we weren't here to pick up the slack. I get tired of cleaning up after these fools. "Oh, I got something for you," he says, reaching in his back pocket and taking out his wallet. So he didn't forget. How did he end up being the only one of my uncles who isn't completely trifling?

"This is a twenty," I say, before taking the crisp bill from his hand. Even when he's smoking he doesn't make mistakes with his money.

"I know that," he says, retrieving the cereal from the table and again pouring it directly into his mouth. He's hopeless. "You're right. Your uncle should break you off a piece sometimes," he says, exiting the kitchen and heading to bed for the forty-five minutes he has left before he has to be at work.

"Thank you," I say after him as I tuck the money into the back pocket of my Lucky bag. I'm glad I didn't have to break off my own change for the bag. Jeremy has no idea how much this hobo would have set me back. Every dime I can save toward getting a ride of my own, I'm doing from now on—no expensive purses allowed.

As I step onto the front porch, I smell a pungent odor coming from outside. I look across the yard to see our neighbor, Esmeralda, staring straight at me and burning a stick of incense. I can't see her eyes, but I can feel her glare through the gate. This can't be good.

"Didn't your grandmother teach you to speak to your elders?" her crackling voice whispers through the faded white iron fence enclosing the front porch of her house. Her birds are squawking loudly in the background and her three cats are lying on the steps, sleeping as usual. They are only around when Lexi's not, which is usually early in the morning. But for any of them—Esmeralda included—it's too late for them to be out and about. I usually hear her outside when I first wake up. By the time I come out, she's always back in.

"You're not my elder," I say, walking down the steps. Before I get halfway down the driveway, she opens the gate and stands there, forcing me to stop in my tracks.

"Don't you sass me, young lady," Esmeralda says. The force of her voice makes me look her dead in her crystal-clear blue eyes, which is my second mistake. The first was answering her question. Mama has always told me not to speak to this broad. I don't know the entire history, but they go way back to their days in New Orleans. And I know she used to harass my mom all of the time when she was younger. As I'm about to make another smart remark, I can't speak. I'm standing still, with my backpack on my back and my purse and overnight bag on my shoulder, unable to move. What the hell's going on?

"What's the matter?" she says, picking up the fattest member of the slumbering cat trio and stroking its back. "Cat got your tongue?" She laughs sinisterly, almost hissing at me. I can't scream for Mama to help me and I can't look away. Oh shit, she's got something on me and I don't know what to do.

"Grrrr," Lexi slowly growls, waking all of the cats up and breaking Esmeralda's hold on me. Thank God for Mama's gatekeeper.

"Meow!" all the cats scream in unison. Whatever she did to me has caused me to have a headache of mass proportions. I'm going to have to run back inside and wake Mama up for this one. I don't want to risk missing my bus, but this is too freaky. Before I reach the porch, Esmeralda and her cats are out of sight, shrouded by the overgrown plants and crap shielding the front door of her home. To be honest, I've never even seen the front door of her house. That chick is strange.

"Mama!" Inside, I call from the hallway as I frantically search for some painkillers in the linen closet that doubles as a medicine cabinet.

"Jayd, what's wrong?" she says, opening her bedroom door, still half-asleep.

"I just saw Esmeralda outside and she choked me up with her eyes and gave me a headache."

"What are you talking about, Jayd?" Mama says, feeling my forehead like I've got a fever. "I know you know better than to interact with her. What's gotten into you, girl?"

"I know, Mama, but she was just standing there staring at me. I was trying to get to the bus stop," I answer, opening a small bottle and swallowing two pills dry. Mama hates when I take medicine without water. She says it's not good for my stomach. But the last thing I want is to have to pee during the hour-and-a-half trip to school.

"Well, Jayd, she's going to do that if she gets a chance, which you can't let her do again. That woman is dangerous and you need to listen to what I tell you the first time I say it, little girl," Mama says, taking my chin in her hand and looking deep into my eyes. It could be the pounding in my head, but her green eyes seem to shimmer, immediately soothing my nerves. "You're going to be late. Let me take care of Esmeralda and you avoid any contact with her, even it means that next time you see her coming you turn around and go out the back door."

"But I wasn't looking for her this time," I say. The worry apparent in Mama's eyes tells me I'm still not hearing her.

"*But maybe she was looking for you,*" my mom mentally interjects, making this a three-way conversation. "*Esmeralda ain't no joke and is powerful in her ability to provoke people. Remember that and she'll never have any real power over you. You just got a taste of what that woman can do.*"

"Your mother's right, Jayd," Mama says, knowing from the look on my face that her daughter's in my head. I doubt she can hear her, but Mama can read me like a book. "She knows from firsthand experience the kind of trouble Esmeralda can cause in the lives of Williams women. Ignore her completely. Now go on and get, chile, before you miss your first bus. And remember, Jayd, never look directly into Esmeralda's eyes." She kisses my cheek and heads for the bathroom. Now I'm really freaked out. So much for my week ending uneventfully.

Jeremy hasn't attempted to pick me up at the bus stop again since Monday's friendly ride. But this is one morning I could use it. I feel drained from my encounter with Mama's nemesis. If I could, I'd sleep straight through all of my classes. But I know that won't work. Today is test day, and the day to turn in my homework for the week in most of my classes. I'm just glad I get to chill out at my mom's tonight. I need a break from both school and Compton. I'm not looking forward to working in the morning, but that too shall pass and quickly, I hope.

"Hey Jayd," Misty says from out of nowhere as she passes our table up and continues her walk across the quad to where the rest of her clique is chilling. I didn't see her on the bus this morning and I didn't notice her walk up behind me. Damn, my senses are still off from my painful encounter with Esmeralda. It's only break and I'm ready to get out of here for the weekend to get some rest and studying done. I've got to find out more about Esmeralda and her powers.

"Chance, get off me. I'm not feeling well today," I say, pushing his narrow behind out of my lap as Nellie gives us both an evil glare. What's that all about?

"You know I'm trying out for *Macbeth* now, right?" he says, sitting next to Nellie, whose demeanor's hella uptight this morning. "I just signed up yesterday."

"Good. Now I have someone to rehearse with. Dudes are always the last to sign up and auditions start on Tuesday." Again, Nellie shoots me a look that tells me she doesn't approve of us practicing together at all. I knew her jealousy would get the best of her once she and Chance got involved.

"Yeah, I know. But can't nobody do it like I do and you know this, man," he says, imitating Chris Tucker in *Friday,* making me laugh. But Nellie's still unamused. Here come Mickey and Nigel and they also look salty. What's up with all of the tension around here?

"Good morning, you two," I say as they take a seat across the table from us. "How are the little love birds these days?" I feel like I've been absent from school for the past two days, since I've been locked in the library when I wasn't in class.

"Ain't no love birds around here except for them two," Mickey says, pointing at Chance and Nellie, who give me a look confirming I'm out of the loop.

"Did I miss something?" I say, taking a sip from my bottled water. I don't have much of an appetite since the pills I took didn't help much to calm the pounding in my head.

"No, you were standing right there when she let that punk-ass nigga of hers disrespect her, therefore disrespecting me the other day," he says, instantly setting Mickey off.

"I keep telling your stupid ass that he's my man and we have to deal with each other in our own way. You don't see me talking shit about you and your trifling trick, do you?"

"You can't say shit about me and Tasha because I treat all of my women with respect," he says. Oh, this isn't going to be pretty at all.

"*All* of your women?" Mickey says. I knew she would catch that, like any other sistah I know. "How many women do you have?"

"As many as you do men," Nigel says, not losing his cool for a minute. They don't know this side of him, but I do.

Both he and Rah can be cold when they want to be. She doesn't know who she's dealing with, and neither does he. Mickey's got all the fire it takes to melt his ice.

"Shut the hell up talking to me, Nigel," Mickey says, rising from the bench, ready to storm off. "Are y'all coming?" she says, putting her hands on her hips, waiting for Nellie and me to follow her.

"I need to finish up here," Nellie says, looking from Chance to her, pissing Mickey off even more. I guess it's my turn to be the good friend, since I've been MIA for the past couple of days. But I really don't want to get involved with their mess. I knew it was coming and I don't want to get burned in the process. They're both my friends. But if I have to choose, I'd choose Nigel's side because he's right. Mickey's man was very disrespectful Tuesday and she needs to be checked for allowing that shit. But she's not so innocent herself and she doesn't want to hear us so I'll be damned if I get in the middle.

"I need to get to class anyway," I say, putting my water in the side pocket of my backpack before getting up and joining her. "I'll holla at y'all later."

"Yeah, go talk some sense into your girl," Nigel says. But there's no talking to Mickey right now. She's vexed and won't hear reason until she's ready. My phone vibrates, signaling a text message from my mom. I forget she can use regular communication when she wants to.

"Hey baby. I have an impromptu tennis match after work with Karl. Can you find another way to my house today? Smooches."

Damn, like I need something else to think about. Maybe Chance wouldn't mind giving me a ride to Inglewood. I know he's not ballin' like Jeremy. Maybe I'll give him some gas money, since Bryan broke me off a piece this morning. I really need to get my own car. Then I won't have to worry about my mom's schedule or anyone else's for that matter. I'm glad my mom's found a new man, which she always does. As good as she knows she looks, Lynn Marie has never had a problem finding a boyfriend.

"Was that Rah?" Mickey says as we speed-walk toward the main hall. She is a good five inches taller than I am, which makes keeping up with her long legs a workout for me, especially when she's pissed.

"No, it was my mom. She's not going to be able to pick me up after school, so I have to find another way to her house," I say, knowing she's not feeling my pain. Mickey's parents have been married since high school, so she's never had to move around like I do.

"Why can't you just stay at your grandmother's tonight?" she says, oblivious to my reality. If it were that simple, then there'd be no issue.

"Then how am I going to get to work in the morning?" Must be nice to not have to work on the weekends. I'm going to have try that one out sometime.

"Damn, girl, I don't know," Mickey says, sounding defensive. "I'm trying to help you out."

"I've got it covered," I say, tired of her lame attempt at assistance. It's time to get back to the topic at hand. "So what's with all the static between you and Nigel?"

"He's just jealous, that's all. Nigel's not able to give me what my man does and he knows that," she says, stepping into the noisy hallway as the bell rings above our heads.

I am and I'm not looking forward to seeing Jeremy next period. I'm still attracted to him because, well, he's as fine as always. But he really rubbed me the wrong way on Monday and I can't shake being pissed at him. I've been giving him the cold shoulder all week and it's not going to warm up anytime soon. "And what's so great about what your man gives you? If you ask me, you could do better without all of his disrespect," I say as she gives me a look of disbelief and then rolls her eyes at me as we approach my locker. Mickey can roll her eyes from here to Compton, but I'm right and she knows it.

"Well, no one asked you. And I thought you were on my side anyway," she says, stopping traffic as she applies her MAC lip gloss in my locker mirror. She's more full of herself than Nellie, and that's not cool with me. As I'm about to respond to her highness's sassy comment, my cell vibrates, signaling a call from Rah.

"Peace Raheem. Shouldn't you be in class?" I say, teasing him. Westingle's a little more lenient when it comes to cell phone usage on campus, unlike South Bay. Technically we're not even supposed to have them on during school hours. But most students keep theirs on vibrate during the day. I usually turn mine off so I can save on battery usage. But ever since Rah and I started talking again, I've been keeping it on.

"Yes ma'am," he says. I must admit it's a real treat to hear his voice in the morning. "Anyway, I just wanted to holla at you since you was on my mind and all. Oh, and I'm coming up there after school, so don't conveniently disappear," Rah says, making me smile with his authoritative yet caring voice, unlike Mickey's man who just barks out orders like the control freak that he is.

"Cool, then you can give me a ride to my mom's." That works out perfectly, because truth be told, I don't want to cause any more tension between Nellie, Chance, and myself. And Chance giving me a ride today would definitely have done that.

"No problem, girl. I'm a holla later on then, shawty. Peace," Rah says in a fake southern accent.

"Holla," I say, mimicking him.

"Y'all are starting to make me sick," Mickey says, as we walk toward my class, which isn't too far from hers. As I approach the door to Government, Jeremy walks up to me and Mickey, who sucks her teeth in disgust.

"Well, good morning to you too," he says to Mickey, brushing up against me as he passes me to enter the room. Damn, he smells so fresh and clean.

"You need to stay away from white boys, Jayd. They ain't no good."

"Now ain't that some shit coming from you, with your man's superhero being Ike Turner," I say, before entering the noisy space myself as Mrs. Peterson glares at me from her desk. "Go to class," I say, lightly pushing my girl as she nods good-bye. I can't wait to see Rah when this day's over. He'll make me forget all about school, at least for the weekend.

Instead of eating lunch, Chance and I met in the drama room to practice our audition scene straight through until the end of drama class—no audience allowed. That pissed Nellie off, but she played it cool by hanging with a still-steaming Mickey and going off campus to eat. One thing she's going to have to understand is that when it comes to this audition, Chance and I are serious about our work and we both want to win. I hope she learns to trust us a little more.

"Waiting for someone?" Rah says, sneaking up behind me as I switch my books out of my locker for the last time. I didn't bother stopping after math class because I knew I wouldn't have to rush to catch the bus after school. And unfortunately, I do have homework this weekend.

"Yeah, this fine brotha who's going to take me to Fatburger for an early dinner. Have you seen him?" I say, allowing him to hug me tight from behind. We could get in a lot of trouble if we weren't more disciplined and if I didn't know better.

"Fatburger? You better be happy with the dollar menu at

Wendy's," he says, dodging my fist as I go to punch him in the arm. After a few playful hits, he concedes and gives me my way, at least for the time being. "Fine, fine. Fatburger it is."

"Thank you for being so agreeable," I say, slamming my locker shut and leading the way out of the near-empty hall. There's nothing like Fridays, especially after the long week I've had. My headache from this morning is still lingering, but thankfully not full force. I'll take something for it when I get to my mom's house. As I rub my temples, ready to release the stress of this place, I notice KJ and Misty talking at the opposite end of the hall. Whatever they're talking about looks pretty intense and Misty's near tears. Why do we give up our power so easily to trifling dudes?

"Jayd, are you feeling okay?" Rah says, following my gaze. He massages my neck while we head out of the front door. The bright sunshine hits my eyes, causing me momentary blindness and my headache to worsen.

"I had a run-in with Esmeralda this morning and my head's been pounding ever since," I say, still curious about Misty and KJ, but more concerned about Esmeralda's crazy ass. Rah's the only person I can tell about my home life and I love that I don't have to explain myself to him.

"Esmeralda your neighbor? I thought she died or something," he says, making me giggle as he opens the door to his Acura parked in front of the school.

"No, she's alive and unwell. She's probably got nine lives like her damned cats," I say, jokingly. But I wouldn't be surprised if it was somewhat true.

"Well, I thought Mama said you aren't supposed to talk to her," he says. Was he listening to Mama grill me earlier?

"I know that, and it wasn't intentional," I say as he starts the car with the speakers loudly bumping OutKast. Why am I defending myself against Rah? "And, you ain't my daddy last time I checked."

"Yeah, but you know your grandmother's serious when it comes to that woman. And from everything you've told me about Esmeralda, she can't be any good." He's got that right. Years ago, I used to tell Rah all about my lineage while we waited for the city bus together. He's always been a good listener, sometimes too good.

"I know. I'm going to ask my mom more about Esmeralda's powers when I get to her house," I say as we drive away from South Bay High. Though I'm ready to grub, I feel like that broad's still looking at me with her creepy blue eyes. I swear she put something on me. I just don't know what yet. But I'm going to find out. I brought my spirit notebook with me and I plan to take very good notes from my talk with my mom and compare them with the spirit book when I get home on Sunday. I'm going to figure out a way to beat Esmeralda at her own game without getting caught in the crossfire, and hopefully without Mama finding out.

~ 5 ~
Things Fall Apart

*"You must've done something wrong/
Why you can't find where you belong?"*

—BOB MARLEY

After we grab a not-so-quick bite to eat, Rah drops me off at my mom's house. It's Friday, and I know he's got clients to hustle for, not to mention a girl to tend to. He also has to pick Kamal up from the YMCA and take him to their grandmother's house in Compton to spend the night. We'll have to wait until tomorrow night's session to see each other, unless he visits me at work tomorrow, which would be a welcomed surprise.

"Hey Mom, I'm here," I yell as I close the front door behind me. The last thing I want is for her to think it's an intruder and grab the little twenty-two she keeps handy. A girl can never be too safe, especially when she lives alone.

"Hey baby. I'm glad you got a ride. How was school?" she yells back through the closed bathroom door. The floral scent of my mom's Caress shower gel fills the small apartment, overwhelming even the fragrant incense burning in the corner. My mom's got Anita Baker playing in the background as she prepares for another date with Karl, I assume.

"School was school," I say, plopping onto the small sofa and putting my bags down on the floor beside me. After the turkey burger with cheese, fries and strawberry milkshake I just threw back, I'm too full to move much further. "How was tennis?"

"It was worth getting off work early for. We had a ball—no pun intended," she says, leaving the bathroom wrapped in a towel with her shower cap on her head. "He's taking me to El Cholo's tonight for dinner. Not the one in Santa Monica, the one in LA, where they have the best margaritas." From my mom's excitement, I'd think this was her first date ever.

"Well, bring me back some chicken nachos if you can remember after sipping on all of that tequila, por favor," I say, teasing her. Margaritas are her and my Aunt Vivica's favorite drink.

"So, what are you up to tonight? Big plans with Rah?" she asks, rubbing her Jergen's lotion into her already smooth skin as the warm light from the setting sun creeps through her second story window, making her ebony skin shimmer. As she props her leg up on the dining room chair, I notice her legs and armpits are freshly shaved. I avoid shaving both at all costs. Luckily, I'm not that hairy.

"Why do you shave when you know the hairs are going to grow back?" This is one of many ongoing debates between my mom and myself. Out of all the things I do that get on her nerves, me not shaving is the one that drives her especially crazy.

"Because I like to be smooth, unlike you, Sasquatch. I swear, sometimes I wonder if we're related at all," she says, leaving the bottle of lotion on the table and heading back to her room to get dressed. "Besides, Jayd, men don't like hairy women. You'll learn."

"Well, I don't like razor bumps or ugly armpits, so if that's what it takes to keep a man, I'm cool," I say, taking my shoes off and stretching across the cozy couch. After eating my big dinner, all I want to do is pass out.

"Jayd, you're so silly. How does this look?" she says, stepping out in a long, white wraparound linen dress and her gold Kenneth Cole heels. Of course she looks flyy and knows it. Her turquoise jewelry serves as the perfect compliment to both her outfit and her eyes.

"You look beautiful, Mom. All except for the naked armpits." Which are clearly visible in the sleeveless outfit.

"Shut up, little one," she says, throwing her wet towel at me. "I need you to touch up my edges and my kitchen," she says, referring to the kinks in the back of her hair. "I sweat out my press and curl on the court." I need to do my hair tonight too, so I might as well start heating up my oven and tools now, even though it's going to be difficult getting up from my comfortable position.

"No problem, Ms. Jackson." I still don't understand why my mom kept her married name after she and my dad divorced. She says it was because of me. I say it's because she wanted to torture my dad by keeping his last name: it's the one thing he couldn't steal from her during their settlement, other than me, of course. But, as they both know, I don't belong to either one of them, just to Mama. And no one in the world would dare try to steal me from her.

"How's your headache?" she says. She must be reading my mind again because my head is banging.

"I need to take something for it," I say, rubbing my head before rising to retrieve my hair bag from the hall closet and set up shop in the dining room.

"Nothing's going to take that pain away, girl. Esmeralda's got you on lock now. Your head's going to be pounding until she feels like letting go, or is forced to," my mom casually throws out.

"I knew something was wrong," I say, plugging the iron oven into the wall socket across from my mother, who's already seated at the table. I take my towel out of the bag and drape it around her shoulders.

"Is this towel clean?" she says, inspecting the various burns and other marks on the oversized purple cloth. "I don't want anything to get on my new dress. It still has the price tags on it just in case I need to return it to Ann Taylor." There's no shame in my mom's game.

"Mom, you know me better than that," I say, placing two hot combs in the oven before parting her soft, thick hair. "And what exactly did you mean about Esmeralda having me on lock?"

"Girl, looking into her eyes is like drinking a cold drink too fast; you get brain freeze. And in this case, it'll take longer than a few minutes to subside."

"Is she more powerful than Mama?" I naively ask. If Netta were here, she'd slap me herself for that question. She is Mama's oldest and closest friend.

"Hell no," my mom emphatically says as she rolls her jade eyes at me. "Although Mama would say that all power is relative. But trust me, anything Esmeralda throws out there, Mama can handle. But why should she have to if it's not necessary? She's got enough on her plate as it is."

"I know she does. I feel bad about waking her up this morning, but Esmeralda really freaked me out," I say, tilting my mom's head to the side, quickly running the warm comb through the rest of her hair now that I'm done with the back.

"Heed Mama's warnings, Jayd. Always. Learn from my mistakes, girl, I'm telling you. It's easier than going the long way around the lesson, which is to not listen and do what you want, even when it seems like the right thing to do. Mama knows things we don't and sees even more. So, let her do her job and stay out of the way by following her instructions to the letter, especially when it comes to that heffa next door."

"Did you ever try to handle her on your own?" As I pull the hot comb through her hair, guiding it all the while with a rag in my other hand, I see the texture of her hair change before my eyes. What was once soft waves is now completely straight, with steam seeping through.

"Yes, Jayd. And that led to my demise. I'm telling you, Jayd, listen to me when it comes to Esmeralda," she says, shaking her head from side to side like she's reliving a painful memory. I wish I could see into her thoughts sometimes. "The more distance you can put between her and yourself, the better." Rising from her seat and checking herself in the mirror hanging on the wall, she walks over to her bookshelf and pulls out her old, dusty photo album. I haven't looked through my baby pictures in a while. From the inside back cover of the oversized brown book, she takes out a thin notebook and hands it to me.

"I've never noticed this in there before," I say, looking at the simple notebook before taking the combs out and setting them on their cloth to cool.

"That's because you weren't supposed to. That's as far as I got with my lessons, but you're welcome to look through it if you'd like. Most of what I have written is about that bitch and how she tortured Mama through me when I was your age. I've got to get something out of the car, and Karl will be downstairs any minute. There's already too much traffic out there as it is and I don't want to be late for our reservations," she says, grabbing a light wrap for her shoulders before heading out the door.

"Thank you for this, Mom." After all of the stories I've heard over the years about how much my mom dislikes the spiritual side of our lineage, I thought she would have destroyed any evidence in her possession years ago. I wonder why she didn't show me this before.

"*Because you didn't need it until now*," she telepathically relays, winking at me as she closes the door and leaves me alone with my thoughts. "Don't wait up," she shouts as she walks down the stairs leading to outside. There are three other apartments in this corridor and I know they just heard my mom's loud voice.

Between my spirit work, schoolwork, and doing my hair, I have a full night ahead of me. I wish I didn't have to go to work in the morning, but I need all the money I can get. Before I jump in the shower, I want to read up on my mom's experiences with Esmeralda. All I've ever heard is that my mom never took her lessons seriously, until she needed them for her own use. I also knew that Esmeralda hates both my mother and Mama, but no one's ever shared the entire story with me. Hopefully my mom's spirit notebook will shed some light on the subject.

March 24, Sunday
It's my sixteenth birthday and Mama says I have to write in this damned notebook and study that big-ass book she keeps in the backhouse. Ever since she and Esmeralda had it out in church a few months ago, she's been acting more strange than usual. She swore she'd never step foot back in that "evil place" again. Daddy says Esmeralda's gone mad and taken Mama with her. I say Mama was already mad and everyone around here is just too afraid to admit it. Miss Netta's the only friend Mama's got around here and she ain't too far from crazy herself. They both get on my nerves.

I didn't know my mom didn't care for Miss Netta. No wonder she never gets her hair done at Netta's shop. I always thought it was because it was too far. But her new stylist is all the way out in Long Beach and she has a standing six AM appointment every other Thursday. What women will do for their hair. But this isn't why I'm looking through this book, and my oven's steaming, so I need to cut to the chase. I want to know how to stop Esmeralda, and fast.

Hmm, now this is interesting. The last entry is two years later and is accompanied by a recipe for a tea called "Things

Fall Apart." I wonder if she made it up herself or got it from the spirit book. I better read up and take notes on this entire section so I can compare the two when I get home.

June 17, Saturday

Yesterday I graduated from high school and I'm done with this house. Tomorrow I'm moving in with my man and we're getting married in Vegas next weekend, even though Mama and Daddy don't know it yet. Mama can't stand him, but he's not that bad. Besides, it'll get me out of this house a lot faster than if I did it alone. Esmeralda has gone too far this time, trying to get with my man. I know, I should blame him for going over there in the first place, but she lured him in with those damn cats and I've got something for her ass before I leave. With all the shit in this tea, her life should fall apart very quickly, and I don't intend to be here to witness it. Mama already got her good, making sure she'll never have any children of her own after what she did to that girl around the corner. I know she's going to be screwed up for life after that one.

I'm also done with this spirit work. I'm leaving all of this shit behind too. This is Mama's legacy, not mine. Once I get married, I'll change my name and start my own legacy, leaving all the craziness behind me for good. I don't care if Esmeralda and Mama go way back and she has it out for us. I can't stand that woman or her evil-ass eyes. I feel like a little part of me dies every time I look into them. Mama already put up a stone shield with rocks on the four corners of our property to keep that witch away from me, but nothing can stop her eyes and I'm sick of it all. I just want it to be all over and this tea should do the trick.

That's the last of my mom's neat cursive writing on the page. From the date, it was around this time she moved in with my dad and things really did fall apart for her after that. The spirit book warns against doing works to harm other people; they could backfire and harm you as well. But I can see why my mom ignored the warning with Esmeralda. I'll have to ask her if the tea worked. It'll have to be tomorrow because I know she won't be back before I go to bed, even though I'll be up for a while doing my hair and schoolwork. But I do need to get some sleep in order to deal with work tomorrow.

"Excuse me," this uppity-looking girl says to me from her seat in the restaurant while her two equally snobbish friends snicker. "Are you going to take our order anytime soon?" Where does she think she is, Red Lobster?

"Uh, no. You have to place your order at the counter and we'll bring it to you when it comes up." These St. Benedict chicks work my nerves more than the broads from Westingle. They all live in Baldwin Hills, View Park, and the surrounding beach areas, thinking that they're better than those of us on the south side of the city. But they're just a stone's throw away from the hood themselves.

"Oh," the snooty girl in their school's letterman jacket says, rolling her well-made-up eyes at me. "Well, can't you just take it from here instead of making me walk all the way back up?" Before I can comment, Sarah steps up front from the kitchen, ready to go off. Marty stuck her in the back as punishment for Sarah sassing her this morning. I'm glad it's almost time to get off. Rah should be here soon and I'm more than ready to leave this place.

"Listen, she already told you that you have to order from the counter. So, either get up or don't eat. Simple as that," Sarah says. Her deep Kingston accent gives the words more power than if I'd delivered them. I'm glad she's on my side.

"Who was talking to you?" the third friend says, but she sounds scared, like she's trying to save face in front of her girls. These broads are too silly for me to deal with right now and not worth the trouble.

"You know, all of this isn't necessary," I say, trying to defuse the situation before Marty walks in from the storehouse in the parking lot. "Do you want to order or not?" Sarah, still ready to charge, retreats to the back and leaves me to deal with the shrews.

"We're still deciding," the lead broad says, symbolically waving her white flag and allowing things to cool down. These pseudo-rich chicks are too much for me. I'm glad I don't have to deal with them on a daily basis. They remind me of that new TV show, *Baldwin Hills*, where I know they are frontin' about having hella cash, unlike in Redondo Beach where the wealth is all real. Before I can begin my clock-out routine, Marty walks in and she's headed my way.

"Jayd, you can go ahead and clean the tables. I'll clock-out your register," she says. Now she's gotten too used to getting her way around here. I hate that she's up in my money like this. But what can I do? Shahid and Summer are too busy planning their not-so-secret vacation to care about what's going on here. I liked it better when they were on the low with their relationship. It seems like they were more cognizant of what's going on in the store than they are now.

"How many times do I have to remind you that it's my job to clock my own register out?" I say, taking the cloth from the counter and wiping down the juice bar.

"Jayd, it's that type of insubordinate attitude that has resulted in your reduced hours," Marty says, laying down a heavy blow in an eye blink. This chick is ruthless if she's messing with my money—and stupid.

"What are you talking about?" Summer has always made the schedules around here and mine has been steady for well over a year. I get my sixteen hours on the weekends and double that during the holidays. I know Marty doesn't have the power to change that.

"I made the new schedule and, in light of your lackadaisical attitude in the afternoons, decided you were only needed in the morning, through the lunch rush." Oh hell, no, this broad isn't serious. What was in that tea my mom made again? If I had all of the ingredients here, this chick would be down for the count.

"What? You have no right to change Summer's schedules," I say, causing the snooty customers and employees alike to stop and pay attention to the scene I'm causing.

"I have every right. She asked me to make changes for the better and I did," Marty says. And, as usual, Summer and Shahid are not around to help a sistah out these days. What's really going on here?

"Look at it this way, Jayd. Now you can get off earlier and have the rest of the day to yourself," she says smugly while stepping in front of me at the register and cashing it out.

"I don't need to get off earlier. I need to get a car," I say, grabbing my things from one of the hooks on the wall and storming out just as Rah pulls up. Thank God for kismet timing. One more minute and they would be calling the police on my ass.

"That's it, I've had it," I scream as I get in the shiny red Acura and slam the passenger's door. His car feels so comfortable, especially with Sade bumping in the background.

"Well, hello to you, too," Rah says, pulling out of the circular driveway and heading to my mom's.

"What's wrong, Jayd?" Kamal asks, touching my shoulder from the seat in the back. "Did you have a bad day at work?"

"More like a bad month," I say, holding Rah's hand, which is already comfortably resting on my thigh. "I have to find a new job, and fast."

"No, what you need to do is hustle your skills," Rah says, quoting a line from his own textbook. If anyone could teach a course on hustling, it's him. "But hey, I got something that'll cheer you up," he says, shining his perfect smile at me. Sometimes I forget how beautiful this man really is.

"Oh really? It's not another song, is it?" I say, teasing him. I love that I inspire him in the studio.

"No, smart-ass, it's not," Rah says, making Kamal giggle. He touches my hand to his lips and drops the blissful bombshell. "I told Trish I want to see other people. Well, not other people, just you," he says. Damn, I didn't see that one coming. I can't even think about getting into another relationship right now. I need to put all of my effort into getting my paper straight.

"Wow. How did she take it?" I say, trying to hide my true feelings and ward off the impending argument for as long as possible. From the look on his face, I've hid nothing from Rah and I feel the pressure coming on.

"She took it. What I'm concerned with is your response," he says. The traffic is heavy on La Brea, making me feel trapped in more ways than one. It's times like these that I'm grateful for the bus.

"I'm a little surprised," I say, only telling half the truth. "I thought you didn't want to give her up right now. What's changed since last week?"

"I changed my mind. I thought you'd be happier," he says, looking at me and not the cars in front of him.

"Rah, let's talk about this later. I've had a long day and Kamal's in the car," I whine. The last thing I want is to argue in front of his little brother. I spent my adolescence trying to shield Kamal from all of the fighting between Rah and their mom. I don't want to remind him of those days at all if I can help it.

"Kamal hears everything anyway, and I'm not trying to make your day longer, but damn, girl, you sure are hard to please." He's right; it takes a hell of a lot more to please me than him opening up his dating options when it's convenient for him.

"And you're hard to figure out," I say, vexed that I feel more pressure. "One minute you're telling me you're not breaking up with Trish and the next you're telling me you told her. What the hell am I supposed to think?"

"You're supposed to think that I love you and want to see where we can go with this," he says, putting his arm around my shoulders and trying to pull me into his chest. I don't care how good he smells, I'm not buying it. Something else is up with Rah and I want to know what it is.

"Yeah, well, I need to focus on me right now, not another relationship with a cheating dude," I say, pulling away from his tight grip.

"Now wait just a minute, Miss Thang," he says in a slight New York accent. He's been listening to too much Notorious B.I.G. lately. "You don't need to be going off on me like this. I'm not the one you're mad at." And he's right. I don't want to have this conversation right now and I told him that. Why don't people hear me when I speak?

"I said let's talk about it later," I say, folding my arms tightly across my chest and staring out of the window. Finally respecting my wishes, he turns up the volume and we ride the rest of the way in complete silence. I want to go home, take a bath, and eat some vanilla almond ice cream to help me forget about this day. And that's exactly what I'm going to do.

~ 6 ~
The Taming of the Shrew

*"It doesn't matter what they say or do/
Don't let 'em get to you."*

—MARY J. BLIGE

"**Y**ou don't have the sight, child," the familiar female *voice says, continuously repeating the phrase with a thick Southern drawl. The mantra causes me to fall endlessly through cloud patches, never hitting the ground but instead gaining momentum and heat the longer I'm suspended in midair.*

"Jayd, remember what I said about using your sight for good. You never want to be the cause of your own downfall," my mom says, but this time it's all in my dream, not her invading my thoughts. I keep falling as the woman's voice keeps chanting her mantra, narrating my downfall. I'm falling so fast that I can hardly catch my breath.

"Shut up," I yell, wishing I could grab a hold of something. Suddenly, Mama's face appears in the clouds, looking at me sympathetically. She extends her right arm as I continue my rapid descent, grabbing my arm which is still sensitive to the touch after my very real dream where I was burned by a fireball.

"Remember Mama Oshune's words: kill it with kindness, Jayd. Kill it with kindness," she says as she smears honey on my wound and disappears into thin air. I flail my arms and

the honey sticks onto one of the clouds, helping me to catch myself.

"Damn," I say, smacking my alarm clock as it rings, disturbing my dream just when it was getting good. I was also getting some good sleep for a change. Between Rah and I arguing and my new bitch for a boss, it was a rough weekend. After my mom dropped me off at home yesterday, I did my laundry, made my bed and got in it. Mama was out in the spirit room when I got here and didn't want to be disturbed. I'm surprised she didn't wake me up before the Tasmanian Devil's rude call, especially since it's Monday and usually my hardest day to rise.

"Mama," I say in the darkness. It's only five-thirty in the morning, well before sunrise. I touch her bed and realize it's still made from the night before. I can't believe she's been outside all night long. I grab my clothes and toiletries from the corner of my bed and head toward the backhouse. I've got to check on Mama before I get ready for my day.

As I approach the spirit room, Lexi is asleep in her usual spot across the threshold. Mama says that her German shepherd is her personal Legba, guarding and opening the crossroads for her whenever she needs to get something done. And I must admit, Lexi is more special than any dog I've ever seen. I swear she's got some powers of her own. Whether Mama gave them to her or not is a whole other matter. But regardless of how she got it, Lexi's got her own game and knows how to use it.

"Hey, girl. Is Mama still in there?" I say, stepping over the large canine as I open the door to the quaint house. All the lamps are on, creating a warm, bright atmosphere in the dim morning light.

"Jayd, shouldn't you be getting ready for school?" Mama says, standing by the stove, which is where she was when I checked on her last night. For a woman in her fifties, Mama looks like she could be my mother's sister. Ever since her hair started growing back after her short cut—which it never takes long to do—people have been talking about her more than ever, saying she got a weave. Mama, as always, ignores the neighborhood gossip. She and Netta alone know the secrets of doing hair, and it doesn't include weaves.

"Yeah, but I had to check on you real quick," I say, eyeing the tasty treats on the table. "Can I sample your batch?" I ask before reaching for the cupcakes. Mama promptly smacks my hand with a towel. "I guess that's a no."

"They're not for you," she says, returning to her hot pot of milk on the stove. "They're for Esmeralda's cats."

"Please tell me you haven't been up all night making something to kill those cats," I say, disappointed I can't try the poisonous delights. I bet they still taste good.

"Girl, no," Mama says, turning off the steaming pot and facing me. "Haven't I taught you anything about character, girl?"

"Yes ma'am," I say, still disappointed I can't take part in the morning snack. "You even teach in my dreams," I say, recalling my falling sensation as I slip off the bench where I'm seated at the table.

"A dream? Do tell," Mama says as she directs my attention to the clock hanging on the wall. "Make it quick. I don't want you to be late and I also want you to write down your dream in your spirit notebook before you forget." I brought home my mom's to study, with her explicit instructions not to show it to Mama. It's funny that my mom's still afraid of her mother, even though she is grown and out of the house.

"I dreamt I was falling and you appeared, slapped some honey on my arm and told me to kill it with kindness, and then I woke up," I say, quickly summarizing it for her. Knowing Mama, that was enough to give me the lesson out of it.

"Watch out for traps, Jayd," Mama says, probing directly to the meaning. Mama's got vision skills like no other. I feel sorry for Esmeralda trying to mess with Mama and for all the other haters she has. But no matter what, Mama's always victorious, like the queen she is. "The ground can give away from under you at any time, most of all when you least expect it."

"You got all that from what I told you?" I say, ready to get in the shower and start my day. *Macbeth* tryouts start today at lunch and I want to get there early. I already know Matt and Seth, being the stage and sound managers, hooked up Chance and me with a good slot, but I don't find out exactly when until the rest of the crowd does. They'll only bend the rules so much for me.

"I've been doing this for a long time. Now go on and get while I feed the kitties breakfast," Mama says, loading her picnic basket with the cupcakes and small bowls of milk. She takes a teaspoon and splashes a minute amount of honey in each cup. "Sweet is always the way to go," she says, following me out the door. I'll have to get the scoop on the mystic treats later. Right now, Mama's got to get on her job and me on mine.

It's weird seeing Misty on the bus this year. Up until recently she's been getting a ride with her new man, KJ. Something must've happened and she looks whipped, like she's been crying for days. I wonder if they broke up. I doubt it, because I'm sure the news would've spread through the campus by now. But why else would she be condemned to riding the bus like me?

By the time we get to campus, people are buzzing around in a frenzy for one reason or another. All I can think about is the tryouts. I'm so anxious about playing Lady Macbeth. I know I can rock the part like no other lady ever has.

"How's my wife doing?" Chance says, catching me off guard with a bear hug. I used to love his hugs. But ever since he and Nellie started dating, they make me uncomfortable and I hate that feeling.

"Chance, you have to chill with all of the PDA now that you're dating my girl," I say, closing my locker door. Reid and Laura look amused as they watch us from across the hall. That wench better not be trying out for my part. I heard she used to be in drama class back in the day, but all of the rehearsals interfered with her social schedule. Not to mention that once she became Reid's girl last year, her identity is no longer her own.

"What are you talking about? Nellie knows we're cool like that," he says, walking me to my class. Speaking of my girls, I wonder where they are this morning. I wouldn't be surprised if they were running late. That's another reason I don't ride with them in the morning: I hate being late.

"Alaska ain't cool like that, Chance," I say as I playfully smack him in the arm. "Girls get territorial with their men, just like dudes. Don't you know anything about the opposite sex?"

"Just that y'all are paranoid. You are way off with this one, Lady J," Chance says, flicking the gold bangle on my wrist before opening the door. I know I shouldn't be wearing this since Jeremy gave it to me, but it's too pretty to sit in my jewelry box.

"I wish you were right for both our sakes, Chance. But you're the one who's wrong on this one." As I enter the crisp classroom, leaving Chance and his idealistic mind outside, I notice our Spanish teacher's absent and there's a cute sub in his place. What a nice surprise to see a young brotha with dreads doing his thang.

"Good morning," I say as I take my seat. I see half the class has gotten wind of the sub and decided not to show up. Normally I might skip out on first period too, if the opportunity presented itself. But I'm sitting in on this class. The new girl looks like she's about to fall asleep at her desk across the room. I wonder what's her story.

"Good morning," the well-dressed teacher says. He rises from his seat at the teacher's desk to write his name on the board, just like a good substitute. Mr. Adewale. Now I've got to get to know this man. With a name like that, he's got to have a story and I bet it's more fascinating than the new girl's, which I'll catch up on another time.

"Hey Jayd, I need to talk to you," Nigel says, dropping into my class right before the bell rings.

"What is it? Class is about to start and I've got a lot of work to do." I've only got fifty-five minutes with Mr. Adewale and I don't want to waste a single moment.

"Rah's been trying to call you since Saturday night. Girl, you know you're tripping, not getting back at a brotha," he says, snapping me back into the reality that I'm not talking to Rah. I'm not impressed with the way he's handling his relationship with Trish. Besides, I was comfortable with the way things were, to a certain degree. Him wanting to jump into a relationship after he was just cheating on his last girlfriend doesn't really turn me on.

"Tripping or not, I need some space," I say. Mr. Adewale gives Nigel a stern look as the bell rings above his head, unlike Mr. Donald, who lets his football players get away with just about anything. I like this new guy already.

"Well, you better get all the space you need by lunch because your boy's coming up here and it's not to see me." Damn, doesn't he ever have classes for an entire day? I swear that boy gets more passes than Nigel catches on the field.

"What the hell? Doesn't he have to stay at school or there's no such thing as detention at Westingle?"

"You should've thought about the consequences for y'all

before you pissed him off. You know my boy can't be ignored."

"It's more like won't, and I don't have time for this today. I have auditions with Chance during lunch, so all of the drama will have to wait."

"Jayd, how can you be mad at him for opening up his relationship to fit you in?" Now, that's about the stupidest thing I've ever heard come out of his mouth, and Nigel has said some stupid shit in the years I've known him. And most of it has been in defense of Rah.

"You see, that's just the type of BS I'm talking about. You can send this message to your little homeboy," I say, escorting Nigel out of my classroom as everyone watches us, the substitute included. I'm glad I wore my Apple Bottoms today because I can feel his eyes on me. "I didn't ask him to make space for me in his little twisted ménage-a-trois. And not only is this little threesome tiring, it's also insulting. I don't need a man so desperately in my life that I'm willing to settle for less than I deserve. So, take that to your little lunch date with your boy and tell him this one's on me."

"You go, girl," my classmate China says from her cannabis-induced haze. I didn't even realize my homegirl was back there, sleeping as usual. I close the door and get back to my desk where I'm ready to study our temporary teacher and forget about the boys in my life for now. It'll be nice to be in the presence of a real man. I need more of these encounters in my life.

"Jayd, do you have your outline for your report?" Mrs. Peterson says, not even letting me get in the door before she starts grilling me. All these people up in this room and she chooses me to start with today. Granted, the class is more bearable with Tania gone, but not that much. If Mrs. Peterson would retire, that would be heaven.

"Yes, Mrs. Peterson, I do." She wishes she could trip me up, but she can't. If nothing else, I get my schoolwork done, even if I have a bad attitude when I deliver it.

"Good. Then we'll start with yours to read aloud to the rest of the class," she says, taking a sip of her coffee without looking up. She's just a shrew through and through, as Netta would say. Just then, Mr. Adewale walks into the classroom with Mrs. Bennett, shrew number two.

"Good morning, class," Mrs. Bennett says, as Jeremy slides in right under the ringing bell. I saw him walking around at break but had to catch up with my girls and couldn't speak to him. As usual, he sits next to me. But today my sights are on someone else. "This is Mr. Adewale and he's a student teacher from UCLA," Mrs. Bennett says, like she has a sour taste in her mouth. Something tells me he's doing more than visiting. I wonder if this was the cause of Ms. Toni's argument with Mrs. Bennett about hiring a new teacher a couple of weeks ago.

"We were just starting. Come on in," Mrs. Peterson says without looking up from her desk. I'm glad to know her rudeness extends to more people than just me. I was starting to take it personal. "Jayd, please summarize your report outline for us, and stand up so we can hear you loud and clear."

"Okay," I say, retrieving the paper from my notebook. Jeremy gives me a slight smile and I return the favor before pushing my seat back and rising to my feet. I want some peace from at least one of my recent exes, and I'm willing to meet him halfway. "My report is on the black queen of California, Califia."

"Now hold on a minute," Mrs. Peterson says, looking straight at me. "This report is on real government leaders, not fantasy, Jayd." Mrs. Bennett looks amused at my embarrassment, but Mr. Adewale looks as if he knows who I'm talking about.

"It's not fiction. She really did rule California, which literally translates to 'the land where black women live.' You can Google it and see for yourself," I say. I first read about her as one of Mama's she-roes in the spirit book, then I looked her up myself and found out more about her. The more I read, the more I wanted to know. "I intend to prove how her leadership was not only revolutionary, but also very effective and progressive."

"Well, you will first have to prove she existed. I've never heard of an African American woman ruling anything, let alone California," Mrs. Peterson says. Now, why is she going to make me go off on her in front of my new man? At least Mr. Adewale will know what he's getting into before our impromptu wedding. Mrs. Jayd Adewale: it has a nice ring to it.

"Well, I didn't say she was African American, especially since America didn't exist yet," I say, sending a chill through the class. Jeremy simply shakes his head and puts it down on his desk. He knows it's about to go down. I guess all of that pride he had in me this time last week is gone. "And also, like the majority of our history, it's been whited out."

"Okay, Miss Jackson, that's enough. You can stop showing off in front of our guest now," Mrs. Peterson says, trying to quiet me down. But I'm not backing down. I have just as much of a right to do my report on Queen Califia as any of these other students in here have a right to choose their subjects.

"Well, I'm actually enjoying the discourse," Mr. Adewale says, catching us all off guard. "Surely you've seen portraits of her mural in the state capitol building? I've read many reports on the black queen of California, but didn't know it was mainstream knowledge."

"It's not," Mrs. Peterson says, shocked at the possibility that I might know something she doesn't. I hate when teachers think their knowledge reigns supreme over our puny teenage brains. Just then, this bonehead from the back of the room decides to take the conversation to a whole other level, silencing my own thoughts.

"Well if that's the case, then why do minorities get all the breaks in this state? If it was ruled by one, shouldn't that make the government even? I'm sick of paying into the welfare system with my taxes." Oh no, he didn't just go there with me. What is it with these privileged white kids? You'd think the money was coming straight out of their trust funds. It's not. It's coming from people who are themselves probably one paycheck away from being on welfare, like my mom or Mickey's family or countless other people I know, none of whom have trust funds.

"Okay, let's not go there," Mrs. Peterson says, trying to regain control of the excited classroom. She picks up her book, using it like a gavel to get our attention. "Look, Jayd, if you can prove that she existed and indeed ruled something, then your report is accepted. Now, let's move on." Yeah, let's. I hate when white people say the word black, even if they're talking about a car. It just don't sound right coming from their lips. But the word minority burns me even more. When did everyone but them become minor? I wish I could be as ruthless as Lady Macbeth sometimes. But instead I'll follow Mama's advice and be sweet, even if I'm the one it's killing.

When I get to the drama room, the audition line is as long as all outside. This always happens, no matter the event. Everyone waits until the last call to sign up, always leaving the regulars wondering about the competition.

"Hey y'all," I say to Matt, Seth, and Chance as I enter the crowded classroom-turned-judging headquarters. "What's the word?"

"Sorry, Jayd. But your audition has been pushed back until tomorrow to allow for more guys to sign up. Right now, there are only two dudes trying out for *Macbeth*, and Mrs.

Sinclair said that's not going to work. So, we're doing the minor parts today. But y'all are first up tomorrow."

"But I'm ready today," I say. I've been looking forward to this audition for over a week and I'm ready to claim my part. Alia waves at me from the long line outside. Judging from her outfit, I'd say she's trying out for one of the witches.

"And you'll be even more ready tomorrow, sweetie. Besides, it'll give you two more time to rehearse," Seth says, trying to console me. I guess I'll just have to wait until tomorrow to be all the bitch that I can be. But I know if Rah doesn't stop blowing my phone up, he's going to end up catching my wrath instead. Speaking of wrath, I wonder how Mama's work is going. I could sure use some of her magic right now because my head is getting hot. Just when I think this audition can't get any more inconvenient, Reid and Laura walk down the hill that separates the Drama Department from the rest of the campus to join the line of aspiring stars. What the hell?

"You'll never guess who's auditioning," Nellie says as she joins Chance and me by the door. I knew Mickey wouldn't venture down this far, not even to support her homegirl. Drama's not her thing.

"Laura," I say, beating her to the punch. I knew Laura would get the bug when it came to Shakespeare; all the conceited folks do. I guess drama's cool as long as someone gets to play royalty.

"And Reid. They're trying out for the lead roles. Mrs. Sinclair sent an announcement request around fourth period stating that we need more people to try out and ASB jumped on board." Nellie still gets to hang out with the Homecoming crew, but she's a lot wiser as to who her real friends are than before. I'm not surprised we missed the announcement. My math teacher rarely reads anything that comes in via a student.

"Unbelievable," I say, stepping outside of the buzzing room to get some fresh air. One minute ASB's making fun of us, and the next they want to be in one of our productions. They are the biggest hypocrites on campus by far.

"Girl, you know they don't have a thing on us," Chance says, joining me outside and putting his arm around my shoulders. Nellie walks up right beside him, staking her claim. "We got this, Lady J. It's in the bag." I'm glad Chance is sure because I feel like I've had the floor pulled right out from under me. I'm going to practice our scene when I get home to make sure my game is tight. But right now, I'll enjoy watching the performances with the rest of the class as soon as the bell rings. Mrs. Sinclair always makes our assignment to observe and critique the auditions. So, I'll have to wait to get home to perfect my own style, because I'll be damned if Laura gets my part.

~ 7 ~
Once a Hater

"Go ahead and hate on me hater/
I'm not afraid of what I've gotta pay for."

—JILL SCOTT

When I get home, Mama's asleep in her room, so I head to the back to practice my lines before working on the rest of my homework and my spirit work. I stopped at Rosa's Cantina and picked up a burrito and finished most of it on the way home. After working straight through the night, I knew Mama wouldn't be cooking anyone's dinner.

I find a quiet corner in the back by the spirit room and get into character, with Lexi as my audience. I turned my phone off to avoid the constant stream of text messages coming in from Rah. Apparently, he didn't come to campus after Nigel delivered my message. I hope he gets it this time before I have to tell him myself. I've been saying my lines repeatedly in my head all day long, but delivering them takes another level of intimacy and I need my leading man to practice with.

Chance is good when it comes to the fun performances, but dramatic theater is not really his thing, even if I think he's good at it. He's not trying his hardest with the male lead role and I want only the female lead—no smaller parts will do. So if I want to shine, I'm going to have to be perfect and that means making the judges see me as a sinister old woman, trying to convince her husband to murder the king.

" 'They have made themselves, and that their fitness now

does unmake you,' " I begin, trying to block out Chance's near-smiling face in my head. Every time I begin my part in our dialogue, he wants to laugh. He says I turn into another person and he can't help but react. I can't control his reaction; I just have to learn not to let his silliness be my weakness.

" 'I have given suck and know how tender 'tis to love the babe that milks me.' " This part of the scene always creeps me out. How could any woman ever think of killing a child, especially her own, for a crown? I mimic the movements of a mother breastfeeding her baby and continue in character to deliver my lines. " 'I would, while it was smiling in my face, have plucked my nipple from his boneless gums and dashed the brains out, had I so sworn as you have done to this,' " I say, feeling the power of Lady Macbeth's words to her husband. Damn, this chick was cold.

"You sound just like that witch," Mama says, sneaking up on me. Lexi didn't warn me that anyone was approaching; her loyalty lies to Mama and Mama alone.

"Hey, Mama. I'm just rehearsing my lines for the school play," I say, dropping Lady Macbeth's stance and relaxing my body to receive her hug. "I'm glad to see you got some rest."

"Yes, child. As soon as you left for school I went down, and I'm just now getting up. That eye satchel you made for me is still working, girl. You've got the touch, chile," she says, eyeing the three cats across the yard. I'm glad Mama likes my work.

"How did they like the cupcakes and milk?" I ask, still envious of their morning treat.

"They ate it all up like it was the best thing they'd ever tasted. Esmeralda never was a very good cook," Mama says, locking onto the cats' gaze with her green eyes. The cats all return her gaze, their eyes turning from hazel to mirror her green. How is she doing that?

"Mama, what are you doing?" I ask, a little freaked out by the extent of her powers. I know there's a lot I don't understand about Mama's gift of sight and I don't know how ready I am to find it all out just yet. When my mom found out, she wrote about it in her journal, but not in depth. She just said she never wanted to see Mama get mad again—ever—and that was all she wrote.

"I'm borrowing the cats' eyes, Jayd. You should try it sometime; it's quite entertaining," she says, her gaze still locked on the feline trio. "The sweets were an offering to them, to make them loyal to me rather than their master. It's only temporary, but it's all I need to see what's going on in that house."

"What did you find out?" I ask, still amazed at Mama's talents. I wonder what that recipe's called and how many other vision sweets there are.

"Well, Esmeralda has some new house pets and she also has some new clientele in her phonebook. And she's also one of those Internet psychics. If people only knew what they were getting into with that woman." Speak of the devil, Esmeralda comes out of her house, breaking Mama's connection with the feline traitors. I wonder how long the influence will last.

"Lynn Mae, you stay away from my cats," she hisses, storming across her backyard to the gate dividing her lawn from ours.

"Stay away from my family," Mama says, now focusing her gaze on the real enemy. The cats crawl inside, looking like they're high and heavy. That's what Mama's cooking will do even when it's not spiked. "I tell you that every time you pull this shit, Esmeralda. When are you going to learn your lesson?"

"Ha! Who died and made you queen?" she says, more boisterous than usual. I'm trying not to look at her, but I feel her pulling me with her eyes. My headache has returned in full force and Mama, sensing my discomfort, delivers the final blow for the evening.

"Maman Marie did! Ase," Mama says, calling on our ancestor whose name demands respect from everyone who hears it. "Now get back in the house and leave us alone before you get into something you can't get out of, Esmeralda." Not challenging Mama's claim, Esmeralda releases her intense look on me and finally retreats back into the house. I wish she'd take my headache with her.

"Are you okay, Jayd?" Mama says, coming to my aid as I hold my head in my hands. "Come on, let's get you some tea to soothe your head." Mama leads me to the spirit room, opening the door and sitting me down on one of the stools.

"Mama, what's really going on between you two?" I say, understanding that this is bigger than some neighborly quarrel.

"Well, you know Esmeralda and I were friends. But the truth is, we were more like sisters," she says, taking a spoonful of dry herbs out of one of the glass canisters on the counter. "We were initiated into the religion together."

"It's always the ones closest to you." I've learned that the hard way over the years, especially where my ex-best friend turned enemy Misty's concerned. If she didn't know so much about me, she wouldn't be such a lethal threat, much like Esmeralda is to Mama.

"Ain't that the truth." As we wait for the water to boil, Mama instinctively begins to straighten up the already immaculate kitchen. "But with Esmeralda it was different. She was my godsister in the religion. Granted, she had her clients and I had mine, but we were always in sync, until I left and came here with your grandfather. But her jealousy had already started to unravel our friendship. When she followed me here it just got worse."

"Why can't you come up with some way to get her to move?" I say, taking the Mason jar full of honey and the spoon she hands to me. She fills the mug with water and passes the hot elixir to me, and I stir in the honey, allowing the vapors to penetrate my skin. I already feel the headache moving to the back of my skull.

"Because that's not how I work. I've always prided myself on being the opposite of what I consider to be evil." Mama sits down on a stool opposite me, watching me stir a second spoonful of honey into my tea. "Esmeralda uses manipulation to gain an advantage over her victims."

"But Mama, you just turned her cats against her. I'm not saying it's the same as people, but still," I say, sipping the brew and silencing myself. Mama looks at me and smiles, ready to break it down like only she can.

"When someone attacks your family, Jayd, all rules are malleable," she says, pulling the overstuffed spirit book from the far end of the table toward her, opening it to the recipe she used for the cats' breakfast. I still haven't looked up my mom's special tea, but I will as soon as I get a chance. "Unlike Esmeralda, our incantations are always pleasant and temporary and always for the greater good," Mama says, reading the ingredients and smiling.

"I feel you, Mama." And I do. I love the fact that we have an inside scoop on asking nature to work to our advantage.

"Yes, but even more so, you need to feel yourself, Jayd. You can't allow her to get to you. That's your weakness. Until you can keep certain folks out of your head, you need to learn how to ignore them." In both the theater and real life, allowing other people power over my emotions leads to my downfall. Mama's right, I need to tighten my A game and that's exactly what I'm going to do.

Misty wasn't on the bus this morning, so I had no distractions to practice ignoring. I wonder if she got a ride with someone. I'll have to wait until I get to school to practice my new skill of ignoring irritating people. I can't wait to practice it on Chance during the auditions. I'm not letting him—or anyone else—distract me today.

"Hey Jayd, want some company?" Nigel says, walking me down the hill toward the drama room. He knows damn well I don't need an escort; he's never offered before. This must be another mission on Rah's behalf and I'm tiring of his crusade.

"I know what you're going to say and I don't have time for it right now. I'm already nervous about my audition and I don't need anything else to think about." Which is why I've had my phone off all day. I'll deal with Rah when all of this is over.

"Who are you auditioning for, Ms. Cleo?" he says, pulling me by the arm, forcing me to come to a halt.

"Nigel, I don't have time for this. I have to go before they call our names," I say. Chance is already down there with the rest of the drama crew. Yesterday's auditions have been the talk of the campus because the witches were funny as hell. I know Alia made one of the three parts hers. All of the other female roles were so minor I don't even remember who all auditioned. But today is the big one and the competition vibe is definitely in the air.

"Just a second. Now, you've given our boy the cold shoulder long enough, Jayd. When are you going to return his messages?"

"When I'm ready," I say, snatching my arm away from his and moving on. "I'll see him this weekend, Nigel. Until then, let me be, please." I can't stay mad at Rah forever, but I can at least drag it out until I have a little more time to think. Right now, I have to make these folks see that William wrote this part just for me.

To my surprise, Ms. Toni is seated as one of the judges. I guess the ASB had to have representation from someone in its camp to make it all seem fair. Well, this may be good for the clique, but not for Chance. Ms. Toni doesn't care for him too much and I know she won't be able to see him as Macbeth. I hope she doesn't penalize me for auditioning with him.

"Okay, everyone settle down," Mrs. Sinclair says as Matt dims the lights, preparing the atmosphere for the main event. I wore a simple white dress and my Montego Bay woven sandals, giving me a very clean look. Mrs. Sinclair always says that less is more when it comes to auditions and I feel her on that rule. "Welcome to the auditions for Lady and Sir Macbeth. We have a number of tryouts to get through, so let's get started."

Ms. Toni winks at me from across the room and I smile back. I have to catch up with her about yesterday's events, especially where Mr. Adewale is concerned. If he becomes a teacher here, I might just flunk a year to stay with him.

"Jayd and Chance, you're up first," she says, taking a seat in the audience as Chance joins me in the center of the room, ready to say our lines. As Matt dims the lights and Seth closes the doors, Chance's straight face starts to crack a smile as I attempt to get into character. I'm trying very hard to ignore him, but it's no use. He's going to force me to smile with him. So much for mastering my new skill today.

"Chance, I'm sorry, sweetie, but this isn't a comedy," Mrs. Sinclair says. Ms. Toni rolls her eyes and drops her pen, ready for Chance to sit down. Damn, he's not going to mess this one up for me. Chance's slight smirk becomes an all-out laugh, causing the audience, filled with our classmates, to fall out with him, me included.

"Okay, that's enough. Chance, you're dismissed for now. Jayd, I hope you know a monologue," Mrs. Sinclair says. This isn't funny at all. I've prepared for the dialogue with Chance, not a solo performance.

"Come on, Mrs. S, I'm cool now," Chance says. But if it's one thing Mrs. Sinclair won't tolerate, it's the wasting of her time. She's got a new man and two babies at home, so I know she's ready to get this show on the road.

"Let's go, Chance, now. You'll have an opportunity to audition for another role, but not the lead, not now. Jayd, act five, scene one. I know you know the lines because you said them all last week in class, remember?" Mrs. Sinclair winks, forcing me to recall the assignment where we had to pick a monologue from the play to memorize. I forgot all about that until just now and she's right. That's my next-favorite scene in the play: the sleepwalking episode.

" 'Out damned spot! Out I say,' " I begin, hushing the mumbling crowd and immediately grabbing the judges' attention. Mrs. Sinclair cracks a tiny smile and that gives me the will to get into character all the way.

" 'Here's the smell of blood still; all the perfumes of Arabia will not sweeten this little hand. O, O, O.' " All I have to do is act like a crackhead during this scene and I've got everyone convinced I'm this crazy queen. Who knew that living in the hood would give me advantages in Shakespearean theater?

" 'To bed, to bed; there's knocking at the gate.' " As I walk toward the door, all eyes are on me. I know I've got this part in the bag. " 'Come, come, come, come, give me your hand. What's done cannot be undone. To bed, to bed, to bed to bed.' " As the monologue ends, the sound of clapping spreads around the room. The applause is contagious and even the other contestants standing outside clap.

"Well done, Jayd. Well done," Mrs. Sinclair says as I return to my seat in the audience. I feel good about my piece, and from the looks on the judges' faces, I'm not the only one. I can't wait to tell Mama how I did.

When I get off the bus in Compton, I can't help but think about Misty again. Her mom usually takes her home after school if she doesn't get a ride from one of her friends first. But she wasn't at school today, and for some reason I'm worried about her. Misty's house is close by, on the way to Netta's shop from here. I could walk down her block instead of the usual route, just to see if everything looks okay.

When I approach Kemp Street, I get this strange feeling, like I've done this before. As I begin to recollect my déjà vu, Felicia and haters come from across the street to be my personal tour guides down their block. Ah hell, here we go.

"Are you lost, little girl?" she says, giving her girls a good laugh. The four of them should really get hobbies, jobs or something.

"I'm not interested in your help, Felicia, so just leave me be," I say, impatient with her bull. She's ruining the high I'm still on from my monologue. As we approach Misty's house, I notice the grass is overgrown and that her trash cans are lying on her front lawn, like no one's been here in quite some time. What's really going on here?

"What are you doing on our block?" Flava, the Latino chick of their crew, says. I see today is one of those days that they're not going to go away so easily. Shit, all I need is to get into a fight right up the street from where my grandmother is. I'll hear about how I couldn't make it down the block without getting into some drama for the rest of my life.

"I was taking the long way for exercise," I say, walking ahead of them and picking up my pace. They're less likely to throw blows on a main street, and Wilmington is only a few steps away. Netta's shop is next to the gas station on the corner and I know they won't try anything once I'm near the salon.

"Well, we wouldn't want you cheating on your workout, now would we?" Felicia says while her followers step in my path, blocking my way. I'm completely surrounded by four girls who hate me just because I'm me and I have no allies in sight. Everyone on the block seems to be oblivious to what's going on over here, but I wouldn't expect anyone to help me anyway. I don't want to fight, but it doesn't look like I have much of a choice. Felicia's been hating on me all of my life, and it wouldn't be like her to let this opportunity pass by.

"I know this hair is fake, just like her grandmother's," Monica, the hefty one in the crew, says as she flicks my ponytail.

"Hating's not good for your health," I say as I yank my ponytail away from her hand, causing L.B., the tiniest in the crew, aptly named after her true hometown of Long Beach, to shove me—and it's on.

"Oh no, you didn't try to get smart with my homegirl. You need to be humbled, little girl," L.B. says. She continues the shoving contest as I strap my backpack tightly around my waist, ready to throw down. I know I'm going to lose, but they won't get away without taking a couple of blows themselves.

"What she needs is a lesson in respect." Felicia steps in the middle of the circle, throwing the first punch. I duck and return the smack, hitting her right in the face.

"Jayd, what are you doing?" Bryan says, breaking up the fight. Where did he come from? I know he's not still dealing with Monica's older sister. I thought he gave her trifling ass up weeks ago.

"Defending myself," I say as he pulls me from the center of the group, where Felicia's still standing, dumbfounded that I got in the only blow. "These tricks interrupted my stroll to Netta's shop," I say, following Bryan up the block.

"This ain't over, Jayd," L.B. says as she and her crew take it back across the street. I really have to watch my back around here from now on. I know they'll happily jump my ass if they get the chance again.

"Damn, Jayd, you're like a drama magnet. What were you doing on Kemp anyway?" he says, glancing back at the scene behind us as we continue to walk toward the intersection. I'm glad he showed up, even if it was because he was creeping during the day.

"I could ask you the same question," I say. We look at each other and silently agree not to mention this episode to Mama. All I need is her worrying about either one of us. Besides, I got what I wanted and got to slap Felicia in front of her girls without getting hit. I'm cool with the whole thing.

"Touché, little queen, touché," he says as we split up at the gas station. I gather my composure, ready to tell Mama all about my audition and about Misty's strange behavior. I wonder if she could give me a little insight into how to help Misty without getting hurt in the process. I also need some advice on how to handle my situation with Rah. If Mama and Netta can't help me, then I'll have to go to my girls.

Walking into Netta's Never Nappy Beauty Salon feels like walking into one of those day spas I see advertised on television. It's the closest thing we've got to one and I feel privileged to have private access on Mama's Tuesdays. I still want to know why my mom didn't care for Netta too much back in the day. But I promised my mom I wouldn't give away any of her secrets. And besides, I can't hide much from her these days anyway.

"Hey, lil queen," Netta says as she spins Mama around in her chair to greet me too.

"How was school, baby?" She looks so relaxed when she's sitting in Netta's chair. Her hair has grown so much that I can't see her eyes through it hanging over her face.

"It was good," I say, ready to tell them all about my audition. "I finally got to say my lines today. But at the last minute, my teacher wanted me to do a monologue and, if I do say so myself, I rocked it," I say, not letting them get a word in edgewise.

"That's great, baby," Mama says, not feeling my excitement. She's never been completely into my school life. She's just glad I stay out of trouble most of the time. Anything else I do is extra.

"Oh, Jayd, I'm so proud of you," Netta says. I'm glad she's feeling me. "What were you performing this time?"

"Lady Macbeth's sleepwalking scene," I say, still feeling the presence of the insane character. Saying those lines took a lot of energy out of a sistah.

"Oh, girl, I love Shakespeare," Netta says, spinning Mama back around to face her on the stool. "I hope you get it. You'd make an excellent queen in any culture." Netta winks, lightly smacking on her Juicy Fruit gum. "Speaking of royalty, how's your little king doing? I always did like Rah," Netta says.

"Rah has been keeping you company more and more lately, hasn't he, Jayd?" Mama says. Why are they asking me about him?

"He came by looking for you, but we told him you weren't here. You just missed him," Netta says. No, he didn't try to invade on my shop time with Mama. Now I know he's tripping.

"Is everything all right between you two?" Mama says, looking at me through the reflection in the mirror at Netta's station. "He said he would stop by the house to see if you went home first."

"Yeah, everything's what it is," I say, feeling a little defeated by Rah's energy. "I don't know what to do about him. Rah's never been easy to deal with, you know."

"Jayd, you need to get your mojo back, that's what you need to do," Netta says as she braids a crown around Mama's head, making me envious of her technique. She's been doing hair for so long it's automatic to her by now. Every time I braid, I have to think about the parts, size, and perfection. And my work still doesn't come out as tight as Netta's.

"How did I know you would say that?" I say. Anytime a woman has a problem with a lover, Netta assumes it's because she's given up her power to the man in the relationship, thus losing her mojo.

"Because you've been listening, girl," Netta says, winking at me and directing me toward her shrine room at the back of the shop. "Go ahead and take one of those love mojos out of the back. Don't give it back until you don't need it anymore." I know who could really use this: Misty.

"So, how did he miss you? He should have seen you walking up the street at least," Mama says, probing into my whereabouts, which I was hoping to avoid reporting. But Mama never misses a beat.

"I actually wanted to check up on Misty. She's been acting strange lately and she wasn't at school today. I think it has something to do with KJ."

"That's not all it has to do with," Netta says under her breath. By Mama's look, whatever Misty's dealing with is pretty serious.

"Baby, Misty's grandmother died," Mama says without too much emotion in her voice. Mama and Misty's grandmother never did get along. "I found out when I looked into Esmeralda's house."

"You mean when you looked through Esmeralda's cats' view of her house," I say, teasing Mama, who's not in the mood.

"Whatever, Jayd," she says, impatiently. "Misty's mama is one of her newest clients, and that can't be good."

"That's the understatement of the year," Netta says, this time much louder. "You see what happened to the grandmother and she's been dealing with Esmeralda for years. That woman is no good, Lynn Mae. You need to show her who's boss once and for all." Netta's serious about getting rid of Mama's enemies. She's a homegirl for real.

"Netta, I can't go around getting rid of people. I'm not the mob. But I do agree she needs to be dealt with."

"What do you think Misty's mom wants from her?" I say, curious about Esmeralda's business. She doesn't seem to work nearly as hard as Mama and she doesn't drive. I wonder how she makes her living.

"Well, I'm sure it's about their house. It belongs to the grandmother's late husband, who's not Misty's granddaddy. So I'm sure they're worried about keeping a roof over their heads. His family already stopped paying to keep the house up. Now it's just a matter of time before Misty and her mama will be out on the street." Damn, that's rough.

"If they really wanted to keep that house, they would've gone to your grandmother," Netta says, putting the finishing touches on Mama's do. She looks stunning and her hair, like a crown. "But they went to the vampire. I swear she's worse than the witches in that play of yours," Netta says, giving us all a good laugh.

"Yes, but sometimes people want quick fixes and magic, which I don't do. So they go to the one they think can help them the quickest and that's usually their downfall." Mama's right. Just like the witches in *Macbeth* misled the king, which eventually led to his demise, seeking help in the wrong places can do the same thing for Misty and her mom. Even though she's being the bitch from hell in my life, as usual I feel like I have to do something to help her, no matter how hard she bites back—and I know she will. After all, that's what bitches do best.

~ 8 ~

Survival of the Bitchiest

*"Your Mama's old fashioned and your daddy don't play/
You'll always be this lovely because they made you that way."*

—OUTKAST

Misty missed another day of school yesterday. I was glad, though, because I didn't need any distractions. The auditions continue for the lead roles and I need to concentrate on both the competition and the tryouts for the character of Macbeth. I'm just glad I don't have to kiss any of them, Chance included.

"Hey Jayd," Seth calls out in the cafeteria. I rarely see Seth outside of class. Even if the students are so-called liberals, many of them still don't approve of homosexuality. "See the results yet?"

"No, I thought they weren't going to be up until after school," I say, surprised at his question.

"Oh, you know how Mrs. Sinclair loves drama. She posted them a little while ago," he says, waving his hand as only he can do. "Honey, you'd better get down there before the crowd."

"Thank you," I say, skipping the lunch line and heading toward the drama room. "Aren't you coming?" I ask, realizing he hasn't moved from his spot.

"No. It doesn't matter to me who gets the parts. My job is always secure," he says. Seth's nothing if not pragmatic.

"Fine. Be that way then," I say, feigning hurt. But he's

right. The folks behind the scenes have stable positions. It's the actors who are vulnerable to getting cut.

"I hope you get it though," he says to my back as I race down the hill.

When I get down there, Laura and Reid are already there. Reid has a huge smile on his face and Laura's facing the wall. I know this trick didn't get my part.

"Here comes my wife now," Reid says, as I move through the small crowd to read the paper on the wall that lists the parts and the names of the actors playing them. He's got to be joking. There's no way fate would allow us to be in the same play together, let alone play a married couple.

"No," I say at the news that I've been cast opposite this jackass. This can't be happening. I check the paper one more time, just to make sure my eyes aren't playing tricks on me and everyone else.

"Come to daddy," Reid says, making everyone in the crowded space laugh. Chance comes out of the classroom door to chaperone me in. Why is this happening to me?

"I just found out. You have my sincerest apologies and con-gratulations," he says before laughing at my twisted fortune.

"Shut up, fool," I say, punching him in the arm. "At least I don't have to be a ghost," I say, making fun of his supporting role. But playing the best friend does suit him more.

"Hey, Banquo is hella flyy. You know I'm going to hook his gear up." Chance is crazy. He's also taking this lightly, to my surprise. Usually he doesn't lose quite so gracefully.

"Well, I'm glad you're finding the situation funny. How the hell am I supposed to play opposite Reid, especially after what he did to Nellie?" I know he wasn't totally to blame. Still, he was the mastermind behind my girl's near-naked exposé.

"I don't know what to tell you, Jayd. But if you're going to rock Lady Mac B, you're going to have to deal with Reid's punk ass for the next four weeks, just like the rest of us."

Chance is right, Reid is a punk-ass and I'm sure him being among the Thespians will be just as uncomfortable for him as it will be for us.

"Did I hear right?" Nellie says from out of nowhere. She and Mickey must have decided to take a stroll down the hill after lunch. I guess they were wondering where the crew went, and since Nigel and Mickey are still at each other's throats, being in South Central must be no fun today.

"Yeah, unfortunately you did," I say, leaving the crowded corridor and joining my girls. Mickey looks completely disgusted, which is her usual expression when she ventures down this way. "Reid got the lead role and I'm cast opposite him." No matter how many times I say it aloud, it still doesn't sound right.

"Not for long," Laura says, her eyes red from crying. I didn't realize she was that upset. "You got the part because you are the drama department's little token black girl and everyone knows it."

"What have you been smoking, white girl?" Mickey says, ready to get up in Laura's face. But I've got this one.

"First of all, don't you ever come at me for being the only black girl in drama, because that was certainly not by my design," I say, ready to slap her myself. But I've done enough hitting this week. I need to try and reason with this chick, if not for myself then for the production. "And second of all, but most important, I got the part because I'm a better actor than you—plain and simple. So don't get mad at me because you aren't going to be in the play."

"Oh, but I am in the play," Laura says, wiping the smile clean off of my face. "I'm not only one of the maidservants who gets killed in the beginning, but I also get the pleasure of being your understudy." Damn, this isn't getting any better for me. I guess what they say about being careful what you wish for applies in every situation.

"Well, study hard," Mickey says. "Maybe you'll learn something." And with that last sass, Mickey struts back up the hill as the bell for fifth period rings, causing everyone who doesn't have stage production or drama class to race toward the main campus.

"We'll catch up after school, Jayd," Nellie says before giving Chance a kiss and following the crowd. "I'm sure Mickey wouldn't mind dropping you off on your special day."

"I heard that," Mickey yells, almost at the top of the hill. "What have I told you about offering my services without my consent? I'm going to start charging you every time you do that shit," Mickey says. But her nod tells me that she's cool with the slight inconvenience and I know her man's still got her on a tight leash, so I ain't tripping no way. Besides, I need to get my girl's advice about how to handle things with Rah before he picks me up from school tomorrow. Knowing him, he hasn't let a little thing like me not talking to him sway him from his desire to see me, and he knows I would appreciate a ride to my mom's for the weekend.

"Settle down, class, settle down," Mrs. Sinclair says as we take our seats and get ready for the play schedule and announcements to begin. "We have special guests today and will be sharing our fifth period with them for the next four weeks. Please welcome Ms. Toni and her ASB class." What! Now we have to be in class with them? This is just too much for me to take.

"Hello class, and thank you for sharing your space with us," Ms. Toni says as her small class fills in the remainder of the seats. "It's going to be tight in here for the month, but we are determined to make this work," she says, sitting in a seat not far from mine and returning the floor to Mrs. Sinclair. It's nice to see two teachers who get along.

"Okay, I know you're wondering why we are joining

forces," she says. I can't speak for everyone in the room, but I know I am. "Well, the truth is, students and teachers alike have a lot of ongoing activities after school. So, we thought it would be best to join forces and hold mandatory lunch and fifth period rehearsals." Wow, they are serious about this festival. It's really not that big of a deal to the students. But I guess these types of events bring in big bucks for the organizations and props for the teachers, too.

"But Mrs. S," Chance says. I knew he was going to have a problem with lunch rehearsals. He barely comes to the meetings we hold during that time. I know he can't do rehearsals every day. "What about food? A brotha's got to eat."

"Don't worry, Chance," she says, rolling her eyes and giving him a slight smile. She's the tiniest white woman with the biggest red hair I've ever seen. "We're having the rehearsals catered by the Booster Club, so thank your parents when you get home for their ongoing support. Now, Seth, the folders please." Mama would never give her hard-earned money to these rich kids to have their lunches catered and neither would my mom or dad.

Seth passes out the thick packets with our scripts, schedules and contact sheets for the cast members, all enclosed in a black and silver personalized *Macbeth* folder: another gift from the boosters. As the class and guests alike get acquainted with the information, I decide to holla at Ms. Toni. The only benefit from this arrangement—aside from the obvious time advantage—is that I'll get to have her in my class.

"Hey Ms. Toni," I say, hugging her around the neck before taking the empty seat next to hers. "So what do you know about Mr. Adewale?"

"Well, hello to you too, Miss Hottie," she says, laughing at my unsubtle approach. "Don't even think about it, Jayd. You know he's too old for you." Man, she can kill a dream quick.

"I know that. But a girl can fantasize, can't she?" I say. And fantasize about him I do. He looks like a younger, slightly shorter Gary Dourdan, dimples included. Only difference is that Mr. Adewale's got dreads, like Gary on *A Different World* back in the day. I hope he teaches in the AP courses.

"No. If he gets the position here, girls are going to be all over him," she says, as serious as a heart attack. "You've got to promise me you won't be one of his groupies, Jayd. All the young brotha needs is controversy." Ms. Toni's right. I'll just have to wait until I graduate to holla at the new teacher.

"Okay, I promise. But don't be mad if I end up his favorite student," I say, still excited about seeing him every day. "So when does he start, what's he teaching? Come on, I want the entire scoop."

"He's starting as soon as Mrs. Peterson retires and will be a rotating substitute until then. He's teaching Honors Spanish and AP Government, and the rest is none of your business."

"So, I get to have him for a teacher? Oh, this day just took a turn for the better," I say. The news of Mrs. Peterson leaving soon alone is enough to get me hyped. I have to get to work on something that will help get her out of the picture that much sooner.

"Okay, let's get started on our first read-through," Mrs. Sinclair says, rounding up the class for our first official rehearsal. I can't wait to tell Mickey and Nellie the good news about our latest addition at South Bay. I know they'll be just as excited as I am about the new black man joining our campus. Maybe he can be a good example and show our dudes how to behave.

"Jayd, are you serious? You're excited about a new teacher? Girl, please. You need to get over this school love affair and soon," Mickey says, sucking on her lollipop as we cruise down the 91 freeway, almost to my exit. "What you need to do is get excited about the fact that Rah broke up with his girl for you. Now, that's some news."

"He didn't break up with her, Mickey. He told her he wanted to have an open relationship. That's still a relationship, Mickey, and I'm tired of settling for his shit. I'd rather be alone any day than be one of many."

"I hear you, girl," Nellie says, taking her head out of her book long enough to comment. "I think he'll value you more if you stand up for your principles now," she says, sounding like one of the shrinks on *Oprah*.

"Where'd you get that from?" Mickey says, looking at her copilot like she just farted. "And what are you reading now? Some self-help mumbo jumbo again?"

"Actually, it's one of two books about why men fall for—for lack of a better word—bitches," Nellie says, like she's just introduced an etiquette book to us.

"You don't need any more lessons in that department," Mickey says, and she's right. Nellie's the biggest bitch of us all and she's good at it.

"It's not about being that kind of bitch," Nellie says, not even ashamed of her title. "It's about empowering yourself in relationships with men. There are a bunch of rules about what to do in certain situations, but the gist is that the bitch keeps dudes guessing, never settling for less than what she deserves."

"Well, I agree with that approach wholeheartedly. Where'd you get that book?" I ask. The look on Nellie's face tells me I don't want to know the answer.

"Where'd you get it from, girl?" Mickey asks, oblivious to Nellie's expression. As she exits on Central Avenue, Nellie gets quiet and stares out the window.

"I got it from Tania," she says, immediately discrediting everything she's said in Mickey's mind. But, I'm still feeling the book.

"Don't shoot the messenger, Mickey," I say, making light of the fact that Nellie left us behind to hang with the popular chicks when she was crowned homecoming princess a few weeks ago. But that's all over now and good information is good information, no matter where it comes from.

"I'm not shooting anyone and I damn sure don't want to hear about nothing that heffa recommended. Who are you, president of the bitch book club?" Mickey's right, Tania was a heffa. But she was also good at getting what she wanted and I don't mind learning the craft from others. I don't want to manipulate like she did, but I do want to know how to get what I want and keep a man's respect, always. Unlike Misty, I'm not willing to give my entire self to a dude, and that type of behavior doesn't seem to keep them interested for too long anyway.

"Hell no. As a matter of fact, I forgot I had the books until I cleaned off my desk yesterday. Now I can't put it down," Nellie says, turning the pages in fascination.

"Well, what does it say about getting a man to understand why second isn't best?" I say, ready to get out of the car and start dinner for Mama. She already told me what to do this morning because she had to get her nails done this afternoon. She's been after Netta to get a manicurist, but knows Netta likes being the only hen in the henhouse.

"I'm telling you, girl, you have to read this for yourself. But like I said, stick to your guns, Jayd. If you're not comfortable with the idea of him dating both you and Trish out in the open then say something," Nellie says, bringing up a good point—and I know Mickey caught that.

"Yeah Jayd, you have to ask yourself why it was okay to be with him when he was exclusive with Trish, but now that he's opened the playing field up to include you in it, you're retreating," Mickey says. Leave it to her to give me counseling using a game analogy.

"Well, first of all I was never cool about being the chick on the side," I say, putting my backpack on my back, ready to push Nellie's seat forward and exit the classic vehicle. Mary J. is softly playing in the background, but the bass is still strong enough to shake her trunk. "And, second of all, he's not opening up anything. He's just having his cake and eating it too, all while advertising it."

"She's right, Mickey," Nellie says, not looking up from her studies, but still chiming in on our conversation. "If Rah really wanted Jayd, he'd break up with Trish completely and wouldn't want to see anyone but Jayd. Now that's a compliment. Making her the honorary second wifey isn't." Damn, she said it so much better than I could have.

"Was that in the book?" I say, teasing my homegirl while pushing her seat forward as she opens the passenger door. "I've got to pick up a copy of that one."

"Yeah girl, you do," she says, showing me the front cover. "*Why Men Love Bitches* is only the first one. Tania was on the second, *Why Men Marry Bitches*, when she snagged her hubby. And look at her now."

"Yeah, she's the biggest bitch out there," Mickey says. "She should get some sort of royalties on these books."

"She may be, but you can't front. The girl's a survivor. Not a nice one, but a survivor nonetheless. I don't know about y'all, but if I'm going to be a bitch, that's the kind I want to be," Nellie says as she closes her door. While I wave goodbye to my girls, my phone sings "Ghetto Story," signaling a call from Rah. I'm still not ready to talk to him. I love him so much most of the time, but he works my nerves like no other boy ever has. When will this love thing get easy?

~ 9 ~
A Thin Line

"It's a thin line between love and hate/
I didn't think my woman could do something like this to me."

—THE PERSUADERS

After a long day of testing and turning in crap, I'm ready to go to my mom's house and chill. I have to admit, I'm excited to see Rah today. He texted me at lunch to let me know he'd be about twenty minutes late. I'm sure it has something to do with Trish. And that thought alone makes me not want to see him. I never know how to feel about being one of Rah's girls. I'm going to tell him I think we're better off as friends for real this time.

"Did you have a nice week, Jayd?" Mrs. Bennett asks, catching me off guard as she strolls past my locker toward the main office. She gives me the creeps.

"I did," I say, not wanting to engage her in conversation, but I don't want to give her anything else to hold against me either.

"I'm sorry that your relationship with Jeremy failed," she says, pausing for a second to let her words sink in. This bitch better not ever catch herself around me off campus. "Maybe next time you'll try listening to your elders," she says, repeating Esmeralda's words almost verbatim. Mama says there are no coincidences and the hairs standing on the back of my neck says this is no exception.

"What did you just say to me?" I turn completely around, slam my locker door shut and step up closer to her. She smells like coffee and cat hair. I've never noticed how blue her eyes are until now.

"Now, now Jayd. This abrasive attitude of yours is just what got you in trouble last time and the reason why Jeremy lost interest in you so soon, or so I hear." Just then, Rah walks into the hall, momentarily distracting me from this witch's words.

"It's been real," I say, walking past her toward Rah, who is waiting by the main office. As usual, his timing is impeccable. One minute more and I may not have been able to hold my tongue. Mrs. Bennett's got her nerve talking to me like that. She's always up in my business.

"Well, you move on rather quickly don't you, Jayd? I knew you were fast, but I never took you for easy." I stop in my tracks, smile at Rah, who knows it's not for him but gives me a look back indicating he's got my vibe, and turn around to look Mrs. Bennett dead in her cold aqua eyes. I know I could take her if I had to. We're about the same height and weight. It would be a fair fight if she weren't my elder. But I'll never give her the satisfaction of having me arrested for harassing a teacher, no matter how wicked she is.

"Easy is as easy does," I say, resuming my quick pace while wiping the sinister grin off of her face. The sooner I get off this campus, the better.

"What was that all about?" Rah asks, taking my backpack off of my shoulder and following me out of the buzzing hall.

"Mrs. Bennett's just hating, that's all," I say, not wanting to talk about her anymore. All Rah and I need is another argument about Jeremy. Sometimes I wonder why it's never easy in a relationship. No matter the guy, there always seems to be drama. I thought I loved Jeremy and KJ, but they both turned out to be jerks. And what I thought was love turned out to be something else completely. And then there's Rah who, regardless of the year, always finds his way into my heart no matter how many times he breaks it. I wish I could cross that thin line from loving him to hating him, but I don't know if I could ever truly hate Rah.

"Oh, aite," he says, pushing the office door open in front of me, allowing me to step outside. The afternoon sun feels good on my face, even in the crisp November air. I'm always hot after dancing in sixth period, so I'm grateful for the chill. "Are you hungry?" Rah says as he leads the way to his car parked down the hill, next to the curb.

"Yeah, but I don't want to stay out too late," I say. I don't want to keep being rude to him, but Rah has to understand that I'm not that easy, no matter what Mrs. Bennett may think. "We can just go to Subway or McDonald's or something."

"Cool. In and Out it is," he says. "Is that cool with you, little queen?"

"Yeah, whatever. And, it's just queen to you." Rah laughs as he opens the passenger door. After I make myself comfortable in his car, I hear screaming coming from around the corner. Is that Mickey?

"What's going on?" Rah says, stepping off the curb into the street to get a closer look. "Oh shit, it's Mickey and Nigel. What the hell?" Rah jumps in the car, starts the engine and pulls off toward the football field parking lot, where all of the drama with Mickey and her man started in the first place.

"What is it?" I ask. But Rah's mind is on getting up the hill as quickly as possible. My phone vibrates: it's a text message from Nellie. I know this can't be good.

"Girl, Mickey threw Nigel's phone into traffic and he snatched her BlackBerry, put it under his tire and drove over it—twice! She's about to kill him. Where r u?"

"Is that Nellie?" Rah says. Sometimes I think he's the one with the gift of sight.

"Yeah." No one else would be texting me right after school, but he doesn't have to know that. When we pull up to the scene, Nigel and Mickey are at each other's throats, giving the crowd of students a free Friday smackdown—no television needed. Rah parks the car next to Mickey's Regal and jumps out with the engine still running. His job as Nigel's best friend is to help him keep his temper in check so that we can all profit from his ass going to the NFL one day. When it comes to fighting—especially with girls—Rah has no patience whatsoever.

"All right, that's enough," Rah says, stepping in between the feuding lovers and pushing Nigel back into his Impala. Damn, I hope he didn't make a dent in the new green paint.

"I agree, you two. Now you're hurting the cars," I say, stepping out of Rah's ride and joining Nellie, who's got Mickey under control—somewhat. Mickey can never really be under anyone's control.

"Tell your girl I thought she was smarter than she looks," Nigel says, spitting on the ground and pacing around like a pit bull. I've never seen him or Mickey this hot before. They must really love each other to be going off like this.

"Shut that punk-ass, weak-ass, wannabe all-star from talking shit, before I do," Mickey says, charging to Nigel's car before Nellie steps in front of her, stopping her in her tracks.

"Why don't both of you shut up," Rah says. I agree with him. I hate when we have to show our asses in front of these white folks around here. It's embarrassing.

"How did this start?" I ask, needing the full story. And Nellie gladly obliges my request.

"Well, Nigel went over to holler at Mickey after practice and they were getting along cool, until Mickey's man started calling, and he kept calling until Mickey finally answered and

lied about what she was doing, which of course set Nigel way
the hell off." Nellie stops to take a breath as Mickey glares at
her, then continues. "So then Nigel decided to tell Mickey
that he didn't appreciate her answering the phone while they
were having a serious conversation and she went off. That's
when Mickey took Nigel's phone and started calling off all of
the female names in his phone book. When she wouldn't
give it back, he called her a trifling bitch and she promptly
threw his phone in the street, and then he got hers and, well,
you know the rest."

"Damn, y'all are too much," I say, laughing at the ridiculous
scene. "Can you two ever just have a normal conversation?"

"We were until she had to check in." It sounds to me like
Nigel's hating on my girl, but he can't have it both ways. Either they're in a relationship or they're cheating. He can't
have his cake and eat it too.

"The problem is y'all are in the gray and no one's going to
be happy as long as that's the reality." Nellie must be quoting
another book because that doesn't sound like her at all. But
I do agree: the gray is never a good place to be in a relationship, which is exactly where Rah put us with his renegade
move with Trish. Now we have to find our way back to some
color, before we go too far, like our two friends just did.

"What?" Nigel says, snapping out of his rage long enough
to laugh at Nellie's rationalization. Chance would've loved to
hear that one, but he's a moment too late. And the crowd has
all but dispersed, continuing their regular Friday routines
now that there's no possibility of bloodshed or ripped T-shirts.

"What's up, y'all," Chance says, not realizing what went
down here a minute ago. "What did I miss?" As Nellie gladly
fills him in on the drama, Rah comes up to me and gives me
a bear hug, sweeping me off my feet. I have missed him this
week.

"Stop acting crazy, girl, and be nice to me. You see what all that heat can do to a nigga?" He does have a point. I wonder if I'm just tripping because I'm afraid of being happy with Rah. A part of it is guilt, but I think it's mostly fear.

"I'm not acting crazy," I say as he puts me down and looks down at me, his hands still around my waist. Why does he have to be so fine and right? "I'll stop being mean to you for now, but we need to talk."

"Nigel, Mickey, are y'all okay?" Rah says, walking toward his boy's car to check on him one last time. Mickey and Nellie have Chance to escort them home, so I'm not worried about my girls.

"Yeah man, I'm cool," Nigel says, taking a last look at Mickey before getting in his ride and blasting Earth, Wind & Fire's "Reasons" on his stereo. That's my song for when I'm really feeling the love blues. Now I'm positive that he loves her. I'm just not so sure that Mickey feels the same away about Nigel.

"All right then, man. We gon' roll out, but holla if you need anything," Rah says, giving Nigel dap before joining me at his vehicle. "Mickey, you good?"

"Yeah, just tell your boy he owes me a phone," Mickey says, not missing a bitchy beat. She's a completely different type of bitch than the one they describe in Nellie's book, but a powerful survivor nonetheless.

"Mickey, didn't you destroy his phone first?" I say, not meaning to bring it up, but it is true. I don't know the whole story, but I do know Nigel, and he wouldn't take anyone's property without being provoked first. And Mickey's just the girl to push his buttons.

"That's not the point, Jayd, and whose side are you on anyway?" Mickey says as everyone waits for my response. Why is she putting me on the spot? I'm not the one who just committed a misdemeanor, even though I have done it myself a time or two.

"I'm not on anyone's side because y'all are both in the

wrong as far as I can see. But you're both my friends and I don't want to see either of you hurt." Nigel, unmoved by my speech, nods his head at Rah and Chance and screeches out of the parking lot. "Mickey, you know you were wrong for snatching his phone," I say, opening the passenger door and sliding into the seat, ready to get my grub on. I was already starving, but this madness has made me even hungrier.

"Yeah, that was a foul move. But he shouldn't have taken your phone either. Why don't you two just call it even," Rah says, opening his door and waiting for Mickey's reply before getting in. I can hear his stomach growling too.

"I don't remember asking for either of your comments. Please keep your opinions to yourself," Mickey says, getting in her car. "And Nellie, you can't ride with me until you stop reading those damned self-help books," she says, blasting Mary J. and rolling off, leaving Nellie to ride home with Chance, who I'm sure doesn't mind the inconvenience.

"That's your girl," Nellie says, falling into Chance's arms as Rah and I settle in for the ride to Inglewood. In and Out is on the way and I know he's headed straight there.

"She was your girl first," I say, smiling at her as we pull off and they get into Chance's Nova, ready to enjoy the rest of the afternoon. I feel bad for Mickey and Nigel. They kind of remind me of *Romeo and Juliet*, in a twisted, ghetto sort of way. I think Mickey thinks she can't leave her man because they've been together forever, and he's accepted and well-respected in her hood. Same thing with Nigel, which is what I also suspect with Rah; they can't give up their links to the uppity black club. It's tragic, really, and I don't want to be a victim of their insane worlds. I just want to eat, be merry, and live life to the fullest. What's so bad about that?

When Rah and I pull up to my mom's apartment complex, I notice that her car isn't here. We decide to take our food upstairs and watch a movie. Rah has decided to call it a night for his clients and to chill with me for the rest of the evening. As we grab all of the bags out of the car, I feel like someone's watching us. Not like when Esmeralda had her eye on me, but like someone's really staring me down.

"Do you feel someone's eyes on you?" I ask as we cross the street to the long driveway leading to the apartments. I keep looking over my shoulder, waiting for someone to jump out of the bushes.

"No. That crazy neighbor still got you shaken up from last weekend," Rah says, reminding me of my headache that wouldn't go away. My temples throb just thinking about that mistake.

"No, this is something else." As we walk further, up approaching my mother's hall, a car I don't recognize rolls by slowly and then speeds off down La Brea. What the hell was that? "Anyone you know?" I say, leading the way up the stairs to open my mom's door.

"No. I don't know anyone who gets down like that or knows where your mom lives," he says, looking over his shoulder before stepping into the living room.

"You don't think your girl's capable of stalking?" I say, putting my weekend bag down on the floor before putting the food on the table. Rah puts the drinks and my backpack on the coffee table and looks at me, very amused. "I don't remember telling a joke," I say, washing my hands in the kitchen sink as he follows my lead and does the same.

"Jayd, do you really think I'd be with someone who's capable of going off like that?" he says, grabbing one of the two kitchen towels hanging over the sink and drying his hands. Men are so silly when it comes to judging women, I swear.

"Now, where have I heard this before? Oh, from every man I've ever talked to, including you," I say, throwing my towel at him before going back into the living room to retrieve my food.

"Whatever, Jayd. Look, Trish has way more class than that," he says, sitting on the couch next to me and grabbing the remote, turning the television on. "And it's an open relationship, which means she can date other people too. So she can't be that mad."

"You can't be serious," I say, taking a long swig of my chocolate milkshake before devouring my box of food. I don't usually eat red meat. But these burgers are an exception. "Not everyone wants to date around like you, Mac Daddy."

"Yeah, but she's cool with it. That's all that matters." I can't believe how stupid guys can be when it comes to the cookies.

"Rah, remember what you witnessed today and you've already seen Trish and Mickey go at it," I say, recalling the last time we encountered his and Nigel's girlfriends at a session. "It's a thin line between love and insanity, so remember that the next time you underestimate the competition." Rah hates to admit it, but he knows I'm right. Rah doesn't like to talk about his relationship with Sandy, my former friend from junior high school, and his baby-mama too often because that chick is definitely off her rocker and he's still trying to find his daughter. I hope I'm being paranoid, but I also know better than to doubt my intuition. When it comes to love, even the most dignified broad can become a hoodrat overnight, if she feels justified in fighting for her man. And that justification doesn't always have to make sense to anyone else.

~ 10 ~
Chickenheads

*"You don't have to kill your dreams/
Plottin' schemes on a man."*

—TUPAC SHAKUR

When I get on the bus this morning, it's foggy and cold. Rah offered to take me to work, but I don't mind the half-hour ride. It's always interesting to see how La Brea changes scenery from Inglewood to View Park, and all the way into Hollywood if I kept on the same route. How money grows in one direction never ceases to amaze me.

"Jayd, I'm glad you're early," Marty says. Why does she talk to me like we're old pals? If I saw her on the street some-where I'd never talk to her or hear her talking to me. But in this situation, I'm forced to deal with this trick in more ways than one.

"Oh really? And why is that? Did I miss a spot on the toilet last week?" I'm sure she'll make a note of my smart-ass re-mark and I'm not even on the clock yet.

"No, I actually wanted to know if you know anything about missing receipts from the register." I know this broad isn't serious. Did she just have the nerve to ask me about my register when she's had her hands in it the entire time she's been working here? If this ain't a setup then I don't know what is.

"Marty, you've clocked me out most of the time. Why

don't you tell me," I say, marching toward the office. I know Shahid is here because his Jag is parked out front. Something's got to be done about this trick, and now.

"We need to talk," I say, opening the office door after giving a warning knock. Shahid says he has an open-door policy, but I've never needed to use it until now.

"Good morning to you too, Jayd," he says, grinning as he counts his cash for this morning's register. I'd love to be in his shoes. Well, not right now because he's about to catch my rage for hiring this broad. "What's on your mind?"

"Marty's trifling management skills, that's what," I say, with her standing right behind me. I couldn't care less about getting fired today. She's already cut half my hours, so I'm seeing less of the point of coming to work every day when I could be using the time to look for another job. The only thing I would care about is that I wouldn't be able to collect unemployment if I get fired, and that would suck.

"Now wait a minute, young lady, let's all calm down," Shahid says, sensing my attitude is a force to be reckoned with. And, this morning, it most certainly is.

"Calm down nothing. Your new manager just asked me about missing receipts and she's cashed my register out every weekend since she took over. Not to mention the fact that she cut my hours in half," I say, rolling my neck I'm so hot. The only time I let my ghetto girl shine in front of Shahid is when I've really had it, like now. If I'm going to lose my job, it's going to have something to do with cussing Marty out.

"Wait a minute, what are you talking about? Marty, is any of this accurate?" he says, putting down his stack of cash and rising to meet our eyes. Marty steps into the small space, standing right next to me, and from the look on her face she's thinking carefully about her next move.

"I simply asked Jayd if she knew where the extra receipts

were from last weekend. I noticed they weren't in the bag with the rest of them," Marty says, quickly changing her tune. Now let's watch her justify messing with my schedule.

"And what about her hours?" Shahid says, reading my mind. I hope he's not falling for her act. Where's Summer? She can spot a liar's scent from a mile away. Even if Summer did ask her to adjust the hours, she would have to be on my side if she witnessed this mess.

"Well, I went through the schedule and compared it to our slowest hours, which coincide with the weekend afternoons. It wasn't personal, but Sarah has a family and I thought she could use the hours more than Jayd." Damn, she's good. Like I told Rah last night, it's dangerous to underestimate the competition.

"You didn't ask me about changing the schedule," Shahid says, not backing down. "Jayd's had a solid schedule for over a year and that's a big adjustment," he says, looking across the desk at Marty and back to me. I know he's asking himself whose side he should take. Men never like to be caught between two women arguing. I know that from living in a house full of them.

"Oh, I didn't know," she says, trying to save face. But she did know after I told her. She should have backed off then, but no. She's trying to shake me and I don't appreciate it.

"Yes, you did, and you didn't say anything about Sarah when you told me last weekend," I say, shocking Shahid. I want him to get the entire picture.

"Last weekend? Why am I just finding out about this, Marty?" Shahid says. Now this is what I'm talking about. Sarah and Alonzo walk in, right on time for the real fireworks to begin.

"Shahid, Summer asked me to make some effective changes and to be firm, and that's what I thought I did," she says, playing on his sympathy and the fact that Summer's not here to validate her claim. If Marty's lying, she's just buying herself some time until Shahid kicks her out on her chubby little ass.

"I agree, we can use some tightening up around here," Shahid says, rubbing his temples and sitting back down in his chair. He looks more tired than usual. "But cutting back on people's hours isn't the first answer to the problem," he says. From what I just heard, I got my hours back. I don't know how I'm going to work the rest of the day with Marty on the same shift, but I feel better now that I've at least shown her that I can't be intimidated. She's no match for me, but I do have to find a different approach to getting her ass out of here for good.

"You're right, I apologize for being overzealous," she says, looking like a scolded puppy. I look over my shoulder and notice Sarah and Alonzo smiling. They give me a silent hand-clap and go clock in, which reminds me that I haven't done that myself.

"Can I go clock in now?" I ask, not wanting to interrupt Marty's fake apology, but I don't come here to give my time away freely.

"Yeah, Jayd, go ahead. And we'll talk about your schedule tomorrow after I have a chance to talk to Summer," Shahid says, resuming his money count.

"So you mean there's still a chance I could lose my hours?" I say in disbelief. How can this be happening? He admitted that Marty made a mistake and yet I'm going to lose my money. What the hell?

"Jayd, I have to verify the schedule with Summer. She's always had the last say, since she spends the most time with the other employees."

"I don't understand. This was Marty's mistake and I could still get burned. I thought you said you'd always have our backs when you hired us. What happened to that manager? You know what, I'm suddenly feeling nauseous. I need to take a sick day," I say, turning around and strutting out of the restaurant. I'm tired of fighting a losing battle, at least for today. I wonder if Rah wants to play sick with me?

"What's up, Jayd?" he says, sounding like I woke him up out of a dead sleep. It's barely eight in the morning and he didn't leave my mom's house until well after midnight. We fell asleep on the couch while watching a movie. We're not one hundred percent back to nice, but we're getting there. He's a good friend first and foremost, and that fact always saves his ass.

"What's up is I need a ride. I'm trying to make a dramatic exit from work and the bus won't do," I say, waving bye to Sarah and Alonzo, who don't look surprised by my actions. They know just like I do that my days are numbered at Simply Wholesome. I need a backup income plan, and fast.

"Girl, you're too much," he says, sounding more awake and slightly amused. "This is why I love you. But couldn't you have caused a scene at lunchtime or something?"

"I see you've got sunrise jokes," I say, laughing at his silly self. I'm glad I have Rah to call on again.

"Ain't a damned thing funny about losing sleep. That's right up there with playing with my money, girl."

"So you feel me," I say, already knowing he does. If anyone understands about not letting someone jack up your funds, it's Rah. He has several investments and he's only seventeen. He learned from his mom's bad money management skills and his dad's hustling how to make money and keep it. Most would call him cheap, but I just think he's good with his money. He could be rolling a sixty-seven Chevelle Malibu—his dream car. But he opted for his mom's used car and has been saving every dime he makes to work on his music and to support him and his little brother. Yes, the brother has his strong points no matter how much he works my nerves.

"Well, if it's about money, time is of little concern." Those Westingle boys sound so intelligent, with a gangsta twist. What am I saying? Rah was born and raised in Compton. He didn't get to this side of town until a couple of years ago. "I'll be right there."

"Thank you, Rah." Marty comes outside and pretends to sweep the doorway. She's all up in my conversation and it's time to step. "And I'll be walking down Overhill," I say, crossing the empty parking lot and opening the gate. I look back and meet Marty's eyes before leaving. If I have to go down, I'm taking her with me.

By the time Rah gets here I've already walked two blocks. It's been a pleasant morning stroll. Older black folks are out walking or watering their lawns. It's nice to see black people doing well. I wish my mom could buy a home over here. But the price of housing is ridiculous in LA, no matter what hood we live in. I still wonder what it's like to grow up on this side of town. Some younger people are outside too, washing their cars for the weekend or going to work.

I'm still processing that I won't be working at Simply Wholesome much longer. It's been such a part of my identity for so long. It's also gotten too easy and monotonous. But that's exactly why I need to shake it up a bit, aside from preventing Marty's evil ass from becoming a permanent fixture in my life. Mama doesn't believe in easy work. She says there's no benefit in sacrificing sweat, time, or anything else if it doesn't sting a little. And this hurts a lot, so the profit I've got coming must be huge.

"Uh, excuse me, miss. Do you want a ride?" Rah says, pulling up beside me. I was so caught up in my own thoughts that I didn't notice him creep at all. I've got to get my senses back on point. Ever since my run-in with Esmeralda last week, I've been off. But I think Mama's got that under control.

"Yes, please," I say, opening the door and getting in. It's not even nine in the morning and he's bumping Mike Jones like it ain't nothing. I know his neighbors must love him. "Your neighbors don't mind you blowing them out so early?" I say, turning down his music. I feel bad for the elders around here. Mama constantly talks about how rude my generation is, and I don't want these people looking at me like she looks at other people my age.

"I don't know, Jayd. But I know you didn't just wake me up out of my sleep to bitch at me," he says, turning the volume back up and heading toward his house.

"Where you going? My house is in the other direction," I say. He looks at me as if he wants to throw me out, but instead he cracks a smile.

"What else are you doing today?" he says as he makes a right on Fifty-ninth Place. "You ain't working, your mom's probably going to be out with her new man all day, and you need to chill on the schoolwork. So, I say you spend the day with me. Or a least let me sleep for a few hours before I take you home." Kamal's probably still asleep and I know it's early for Rah to be up and out.

"Okay, fine," I say. "But I'm not cooking." The last time I spent the day with him and Nigel, I ended up making a five-course breakfast for us while they played video games all morning. That was the last time I ditched with them.

"Cool. Just braid a brotha's hair, please," he says, pulling into his driveway and turning the car off. I get out and head up the front steps as Rah follows and grabs me from behind, hugging me tight.

"I'm wide awake now," he says, and he's definitely excited to see me. "Miss me this week?"

"Not that much," I say, pushing his hands from around me and stepping away. "Don't start no shit, Rah," I say as he opens the door, letting me in first.

"Why not," he says, bending down and kissing me hard. It does feel good, I admit. But Rah has a habit of feeling too good, and I don't want to go to the point of no return. Besides, he's not done with Trish and I'm not sharing this part of our relationship with her. Oh, but he kisses so nice.

"Just let go, Jayd. You know you want to," he says, coming up for air. How come when KJ said the same words they infuriated me? But coming from Rah's mouth it sounds so sweet. "You can trust me now."

"What!" I say, backing away from his lethal lip lock, sobering up just in time to set him straight. "How can I trust you when you're still with Trish?"

"It's an open relationship, Jayd. Why can't you accept that?" He sounds both sincere and stupid.

"Because you didn't discuss it with me," I say. I don't want to argue with him right now, but it's all coming out and I'm going to let it flow. "You thought that my only issue was that I couldn't be your girlfriend, so you made me one of your girlfriends, thinking that would make me happy—and that's insulting. You should know me better than that by now," I say, following him into the studio. He switches the lights on low and grabs the remote for the sound system. Sam Cook's melodic voice creeps out of the speakers, putting us in a mellower mood. It's been an intense morning and I just want to chill for a little while.

"I'm sorry, but I didn't know what else to do. You know I hate hurting people," he says, taking a seat next to me on the couch. He grabs the herb box on the table and opens it, taking out a half-smoked blunt and a lighter. After a few puffs he passes it to me, knowing I don't smoke.

"Are you that high already?" I say, still waiting for him to get back to the topic on the floor.

"No, but it'll mellow you out. Besides, you ain't got no job and you ain't got shit to do," Rah says, mimicking Chris Tucker.

"This ain't *Friday*, fool," I say, pushing his hand away and making myself comfortable in the cozy room. I could use a nap myself, and the inevitable high from Rah's smoke will help me rest well.

"Nah, but it's still good medicine for a stressful situation." Rah is so silly sometimes. Unlike him, I don't want to chill when it comes to certain issues, like Trish.

"Look, I never asked you to choose between me and Trish, because I knew you weren't ready to let that go," I say, not even wanting to sound like I care about the trick. My only concern in this situation is me and my feelings. To hell with anyone else right now. "And I'm cool with that. But don't make me a target for the girl to come after. And that's exactly what you've done by opening your relationship up."

"How, when it's a compromise? I was planning on breaking up with her, but I know that would crush her and it's the beginning of the school year, too. It's bad timing for her socially, you feel me?" Ah, a private insight into the social logic of Westingle.

"No, I don't. But, that's not my concern. I say we stay friends that flirt. It's easier than trying to build a relationship on a weak foundation." His look of recognition says I've made my point. His droopy eyes say it's time to stop talking and take a rest.

"You still braiding my hair when we wake up, right?" Rah says, stretching his legs across the couch and laying his head in my lap. He's nothing if not confident.

"Yeah, I'll hook you up." As I doze off, I can't help but wonder how we got to this point. And where can we go from here?

* * *

After sleeping the rest of the morning and a good chunk
of the afternoon away, Rah and I wake up and eat like we
haven't had a morsel of food all week. After lunch, we get
busy braiding, and Rah can also get a little work done, but
not before I finish my grill from earlier. I'm wide awake now
and ready to hash it out some more. I want him to understand fully where I'm coming from.

"Rah, why can't we go to the movies or just go hang somewhere?" That's one of the things I miss most about my relationship with Jeremy. He would take me out every weekend. All
Rah and I ever do is sit up in the house or at the studio, and
that's getting to be a bit tedious.

"Because I have to work on the weekends, Jayd. You know
this," he says, bending his head so I can get the part straight.
His new beat fills the room, making it difficult to have a conversation, and I know he's doing it on purpose.

"Rah, can you tone it down, please? I'm trying to talk to
you," I say, greasing his scalp before I pull the braid into
shape. I'm almost finished with his head and want to go back
to my mom's after I'm done. It's almost four now and I want
to go home, shower and change before we hang out this
evening.

"Jayd, haven't we talked enough this morning?" he says,
reluctantly turning the music down. "And we do go out. Didn't
I take you out to eat last night?"

"You call going to a drive thru going out?" I say, smacking
him in the head with the hard comb before parting my next
braid. "Are you ashamed of me or something?"

"No, girl, come on," he says, bending his head back into
my thighs and looking up at me. "I could never be ashamed
of you." As Rah straightens his neck and I continue to braid, I
can't help but wonder if Trish knows he's still courting me.
I'm sure she's both suspicious and jealous. And if I know
anything about chickenheads it's that they cluck loudest

when they feel threatened; Trish has already proven that to be true.

"Rah, does Trish know you're trying to make me wifey number two?" I ask. His entire upper body tenses while my fingers work their magic on his scalp. Normally he'd be melting like butter by now.

"She knows we're building," he says, expertly evading a straight answer. "And that's all she needs to know. What we do is our business," he says, caressing my ankles as I finish the last braid.

"Then why can't we go out and kick it on a real date?" Pushing his head forward, I swing my right leg over him and rise from the couch. I have been sitting for over an hour and need to move around. "Come on, take me to the marina."

"No, Jayd," he says sternly. His look is so serious it gives me the chills.

"What aren't you telling me?" I say, standing over him and forcing him to look up at me. "You really didn't tell her you wanted an open relationship, did you?" If this boy is lying I swear I'm never talking to him again—ever.

"Trish knows what's up, Jayd. But, like I said, I don't like hurting people and she's been through a lot with me, just like you have."

"Then what is it? And tell me the truth." As the saying goes, silence is golden and Rah's speechlessness has hit the jackpot for me. Whatever he isn't saying is big.

"Look, I just don't want it getting back to Trish where we are and what we do," he says. I know he's not telling me he can't take me out because he's afraid of what people will say. What the hell?

"So she gets to be the public wifey and I get the studio time, is that it?" I knew it was too good to be true. He came back into my life, making me fall for him all over again, only to keep me on a string and never allow me in all the way.

"No, that's not it at all," he says, getting up and taking my hands, forcing me to look at him through my tears. "Look, Jayd, I'm just trying to protect you. You have to trust me on this one. Now isn't the right time to show you off to the world. Otherwise there would be no need to compromise at all. You'd be my queen in the studio, at the marina and everywhere else."

"What does she have on you?" I ask. I know she knows about his hustling, but I wonder if she has anything to do with it.

"Her older brother is my main supplier," he says, finally telling the whole truth. I knew she wasn't but a stone's throw away from being a hoodrat. Got damn, I knew it was something big, but not like this. "And she's literally shed blood for me dealing with my baby-mama drama, so she's not going to go away just because I'm not feeling her like I used to."

"Yeah, I guess not after all that y'all have been through together," I say, trying to be sympathetic. But I don't like my friend being forced to stay in a relationship he doesn't want; I don't care who her brother is. In my hood, intimidation only works on the weak and none of my friends are weak. And even in their time of need, my friends have a secret weapon they don't even know about: me. When I get home tomorrow, I'm going to get to work on helping both Rah and Misty see their way out of their individually tangled webs.

~ 11 ~
Not In My Hood

*"If the road to the riches lead through my hood/
Then it's best you change y'alls route."*

—BOYZ N DA HOOD

When my mom picked me up from work, I was worn out. Marty was a bigger bitch than ever today and Summer and Shahid were nowhere around to help. I'm ready to get home and chill out for the rest of the evening, even if chilling in my world means catching up on my school and spirit work. Mama's been so distracted by Esmeralda that she hasn't given me any new lessons. But I'm still working on the power of my thoughts assignment she gave me last time. I think I'm getting the hang of it, at least the thinking part. Silently observing is still a challenge for me.

"Have you told Mama about Karl yet?" my mom asks as she pulls up to Mama's house. We haven't spent much time together since her new man landed in our lives, but she seems genuinely happy this time around, so I'm done hating on her. She's lucky I'm a good girl. Otherwise her apartment would be party central, as much as she leaves me alone in it.

"No, I didn't think you wanted me to say anything," I say, grabbing my bags from the back. "Has that changed?"

"Well, I'm going to tell her in my own time. Karl's different, and I don't want to jinx it, but I think he may be here to stay." My mom sounds like she's my age and talking about her first love. I've never seen her so giddy before. It's almost sickening, especially since my love life is so tumultuous all of the time. Am I going to have to wait until I'm in my thirties to find true and stable love?

"*Maybe, you never know. But the blessing is in finding love at all*," my mom says, looking at me and smiling, never actually saying a word.

"Does your man know he can't hide his thoughts from you?" I say. She rests her head on the soft gray headrest and looks out of the window. The neighbors are wrapping up their Sunday evening duties of watering the grass and catching up on the weekend gossip.

"Jayd, you'll soon find out, if you don't already know, that men can only handle so much information," she says, turning to face me. The setting sun makes her green eyes even more luminous. I'm sure Karl doesn't have any complaints about the Lynn Marie he knows and loves. "*You've got that right*."

"If it gets serious, you're going to have to tell him eventually." My mom's the queen of secret-keeping. And, like most secrets, they always find a way out.

"Hell no, I don't have to tell him a damned thing," she says. "Look, Jayd, I'm not like you. I don't get into our lineage like you do and I can't use my powers on anyone else but you, so this really doesn't affect him at all." Mama steps out of the house and onto the front porch, looking toward Esmeralda's house, until she notices us sitting in the car in the driveway.

"Lynn Marie, were you planning on coming in to say hello this time, or just do a drop-off like you did last weekend?" Mama asks. "You should at least come greet the family shrine every now and again."

"Hi Mama," my mom says, rolling her eyes. She's lucky Mama can't see her clearly because I know she'd get a slap for that one, no matter how old she is. "I was in a hurry last

Sunday and this one too. So, Jayd, get to scooting. I'll see you next weekend, baby," she says, giving me a kiss on the cheek before pushing me out of her car. "And Jayd, you can keep our talk between us, if you catch my drift." Loud and clear, and I know she heard me.

"How was your weekend, baby?" Mama says from the porch where she's picking the dead petals off her roses. Daddy doesn't do much around the house if it doesn't involve working on his cars. But the one thing he does for Mama is keep the yard up.

"It was okay. Work sucked, but what else is new," I say, making my way up the driveway to give Mama a hug.

"And, how's your mother's new man?" she says, like we've talked about Karl before, and I know my mom hasn't told her anything. Mama's good at fishing for information. I can't lie to Mama and I can't rat my mom out. What do I do?

"You know my mom doesn't talk to me about that kind of stuff," I say, passing Mama to go into the house. "It smells like fried fish and hush puppies in here." I love it when Mama makes fish. Her batter is gold, flaky and sweet and the fish is always juicy. She must've gone fishing with Netta this morning. That also means there was some spiritual work done. Mama never goes to the river, lake or any other body of water without bringing something for Oshune.

"Jayd, you didn't answer me, and I know your mom talks to you or around you about her men," Mama says, passing me up in the dining room to enter the kitchen. She takes the last of the sizzling round hush puppies out of the cast iron skillet and places them on the plate covered in paper towels. I put my bags down on the dining room floor and wash my hands in the sink. "I'm worried about my daughter. All you have to do is answer me and I won't be worried anymore." Damn, she's good.

"They're very happy and that's all I know," I say, taking

one of the golden brown hush puppies and popping it into my mouth. "Mama, you put your foot in this food," I say, taking another one and then looking into the other five covered plates on the table. She's got enough food here to feed the household, but I already know it's not for them. Daddy's probably eating dinner at the church and who knows where my uncles are.

"What's up, Jayd," my cousin Jay says as he enters the kitchen, rubbing his belly. "Something smells good in here."

"Jay, go wash up and get ready to eat before I serve this food up," Mama says, exiting the kitchen to get her good dishes out of the china cabinet and coming back into the kitchen. "Jayd, wash these plates so we can feed the ancestors and Orisha before we eat."

"Yes ma'am." I reluctantly take the heavy plates and put them in the sink. I want to throw down now. How come Jay gets to sleep all day and as soon as I walk in the door, Mama's got work for me?

"What's that look on your face, Jayd?" Mama says, dishing out rice and vegetables on a plate—for Jay, I assume.

"Mama, how come you didn't tell Jay to wash the dishes?" I already know she's going to say I'm whining or something like that. But I'm tired of the men skating on easy around here—and everywhere else, from what I can see.

"Girl, stop complaining and dry those dishes off. Here's your plate, Jay. Make it good because that's all you're getting," she says, passing him his dinner. He attempts to come in the kitchen, but Mama blocks his way.

"Can a brotha at least get some hot sauce?" he says. Mama opens the cabinet above the counter and passes him a bottle of Red Rooster. "Thank you," he says, taking his usual seat on the couch to watch MTV for the remainder of the evening. I hardly ever get to watch television when I'm here. Jay never brings home any homework on the weekends, unlike myself.

I don't believe that Compton High doesn't give it out as much as Jay chooses not to do it. He's probably the most nonchalant teenager I know.

"Jayd, we've got work to do. I know you feel like I make you work harder than the boys and you're right," she says, taking the three clean plates and putting them on the table before piling them with food. "I expect more from you because the world does. So get used to constantly working: that's what women do, especially mothers." I knew I should've kept my mouth shut. Mama gives no sympathy when it comes to getting work done.

"Can I eat dinner?" I ask. Mama stops what she's doing, puts her hands on her hips and gives me a look that says, "I know you didn't ask me that silly-ass question."

"Pick up the plates and take them to the shrine." I follow Mama into her room and put the plates down on the floor beside Mama's bed. She's decorated the shrine lavishly in hues of orange, yellow, and gold for our deity, Oshune. There are also two mini shrines on the floor: one is all white and the other is decorated with red and black cloth.

"Mama, who are these for?" I ask, placing a plate of food on each shrine, as her finger directs exactly what goes where.

"You tell me," she says, giving me an impromptu quiz. She never quits. "When we feed the ancestors, what colors do we use?"

"White and silver," I say. That was easy, and one of the first lessons I learned when I started studying with Mama.

"Very good," she says as I walk around her bed and stand next to mine, watching as Mama lights the yellow and white candles on the shrine. She takes a red candle out and puts it next to the red and black shrine on the floor. I notice there is also a stone figure with three cowry shells inside it, sitting on a clay plate and decorated with candy and toys.

"Mama, that is new. Who's it for?" I ask, ready to go back

into the kitchen and fix my own plate. But the shrine looks beautiful and she's done a lot of work to it over the weekend. I know it has something to do with Esmeralda.

"That's Legba, my father Orisha," she says, smiling as she bends down to put the tall seven-day candle on the floor next to the clay plate. "He opens the roads, moves obstacles, and much, much more." Now I see the connection: she wants to get Esmeralda out of the neighborhood for good. I knew Mama would handle it like only she can.

"That's what I'm talking about, Mama. Can he help a sistah out? I've got some roads and obstacles to deal with myself."

"Of course he can, baby. You've got to be ready for the sacrifice, though. There is no gain without giving. Netta and I have been working all weekend to get rid of the negative energy around this house," she says, glancing in the direction of Esmeralda's house. "I'm begging for that woman to be forced out of here, one way or another."

"I will help in any way that I can," I say, following Mama back into the kitchen to eat our dinner, I hope.

"You can help by studying your lessons and keeping out of Esmeralda's sight—literally. Help yourself to the food, Jayd. The rest of this feast is ours."

I'm happy to study my lessons tonight. My plan is to camp out in the spirit room for the rest of the evening. I'm determined to help Rah get out of his relationship with Trish and keep his head on his shoulders. I don't know anything about her brother, but if he's anything like her, I don't like him already. I also want to see if there's anything I can do to help Misty out. She's far from my favorite person. But if her family's involved with Esmeralda in any way, Misty needs my help, whether she knows it or not.

* * *

The usual suspects are hanging at the bus stop this morning, leaving no space for me to rest my weary bones. I stayed up until midnight working on my schoolwork and searching through the spirit book for some guidance. I finished my homework, but I need to keep looking for something to help Misty and Rah out of their self-made hells. Speak of the devil, Misty's taking my bus this morning. Usually she catches the bus off of Central rather than walk up to Wilmington like I do. It's a longer stroll, but it's more peaceful and I can avoid sitting with Misty for at least one of the three rides.

"Good morning," I say as she stands next to me. There are several people around and I know her well enough to know she doesn't like to be alone in a crowd.

"Why are you talking to me?" Misty says. And, I have to agree. Why am I talking to her?

"I heard about your grandmother and I wanted to offer my condolences for you and your mother." That's enough talking for now, and she can stand alone for all I care. Before I walk over to the other side of the stop, I notice Misty's eyes look sunken, like she hasn't slept or eaten in days. I wonder how she's really doing and how much longer she and her mom will be able to stay in their house. With her grandmother's passing, they have no legal rights to the house and will be out on the streets soon. I know her mom doesn't make much as a part-time secretary at our school, so she won't be able to pay the rent alone. And Misty getting a job is out of the question because she doesn't like manual labor, as she calls it.

"Jayd," Misty says. I turn back and look down at her. I almost forgot she makes my short-ass feel tall. "Thank you," she says as the bus rolls up. Misty takes out her bus pass and passes me up to get in line. Her thank you was sincere and her eyes sad. Now I feel even more of an urgency to help the girl out. But, knowing Misty, she won't make it easy.

"Did you have to take the bus with her again?" Mickey says, snacking on bag of popcorn before the bell rings. It's been a slow Monday so far. But it's only break and anything's bound to happen.

"Yes, I did. I don't know what's going on with her and KJ. If that's his girl, shouldn't he be giving her a ride?"

"Now you know that was never his girl," Nellie says, completely engulfed in her bitch book, but not too preoccupied to keep up with the conversation.

"Yeah, there's a big difference between a girlfriend and a ho." Damn, Mickey has no love for Misty whatsoever, and I can't blame her. They've been enemies the entire time we've been at Drama High.

"There's KJ now. Why don't you ask him why he can't give Misty a ride anymore?" Nellie says, laughing at her own joke. But KJ looks anything but funny as he walks up to Misty and grabs her by the arm, snatching her up out of her seat and shocking everyone around South Central. What the hell?

"Where the hell have you been?" KJ shouts at her. I guess he's in the dark just like the rest of us. "I've been calling you all weekend. Didn't you get my messages?"

"Damn, KJ man, back off," C Money says as he and Del step in between Misty and their boy. Something's not right with Misty, and it's more than her grandmother's passing. She seems out of it, like she's not in her body or something. I know her well enough to know she wouldn't normally allow anyone to touch her like that without saying something, not even her beloved KJ.

"I'll be right back, y'all," I say, rising from our bench and marching over to South Central. I know this is none of my business, but this fight is unfair and Misty doesn't have any girls to back her up. I can't watch her get humiliated like this, especially when she's not herself.

"Jayd, what are you doing? I know you're not going to help that girl," Mickey calls out after me. But I'm on a mission. I don't care if everyone else around me wants to see the drama unfold. I'm not standing by and watching nobody get beat down unfairly, especially not a girl by a dude. I don't see how my neighbors at home can stand by and watch when my uncles get into it. I'm like Mama when it comes to most things, especially abuse. And, like she says, I don't care what people do when they go home, but I'll be damned if I'll watch someone suffer in my hood.

"KJ, why don't you pick on someone your own size," I say. Everyone's staring at me while I stand by Misty's side as his boys try and calm him down. By the look in KJ's eyes, I've just added fuel to his fire.

"Did I miss something?" Shae says from her table where she and her silent man, Tony, are seated. "When did you become Misty's cheerleader?"

"The real question is, why aren't you?" I say, not backing down from the queen of this clique. Thank God I've never been a member.

"Why don't you mind your business," KJ says, still holding Misty's arm. She hasn't moved a muscle. I need to get her out of here and fast.

"Any time a dude feels like snatching up a girl, it is my business," I say, putting my hand on top of his. The bell rings and everyone is frozen in place, waiting to see what will happen next.

"Jayd, back off," KJ says, taking his other hand and removing mine from his. He should know better than to try and scare me. I put my hand back on his and grab it tightly. If I had Mickey's nails, he'd be bleeding by now.

"Go to class, KJ," I say. Everyone around gasps as the tension rises and Misty's still motionless. Chance and Nigel come over from the main quad and stand behind me. Nellie and Mickey follow suit. KJ, noticing the vibe is out of his control, finally lets go and storms off to class.

"I hope you know what you're doing," Mickey says as they head to class.

"You should talk," Nigel says to Mickey, and they are at it again. I can't get caught up in their drama today. I have to figure out a way to help Misty, and fast. She's in no condition to be at school. I know her mom didn't come to work again today, so how am I going to get this girl home? Mama. If I call her and tell her I need to come home and bring Misty with me, she'll know it's an emergency—no questions asked. And that's just what I'm going to do.

"Get that girl in here now," Mama says, meeting us on the porch and cloaking Misty in a blanket. It's a chilly day and Misty's dressed like it's summertime. "What happened to her?" When Misty walks into our house, she sits down on the couch and looks around the room. It's as if she's never been to my house before, even though she used to hang out here often when we were friends. Everything seems new to her.

"I don't know, but she's not herself at all." Mama takes one look at Misty and sits down on the couch. She looks worried and scared at the same time. I've never seen Mama look like this before. Something must be very wrong to turn Mama gray.

"Esmeralda," Mama whispers. Her eyes wander out the window, staring at her enemy's house. She's got to be the one to leave the neighborhood, not Misty. I know Mama's got more tricks up her sleeve than she reveals, and so do I. I don't know what they are yet. But I'm going to find out before I go to sleep tonight. Enough is enough.

~ 12 ~
Trickin'

"I'm trickin' and I ain't making five hundred dollars/
What the hell fool?"

—LEXUS/*HUSTLE & FLOW* SOUNDTRACK

Mama's been in the spirit room for over an hour. She told me to stay with Misty, who's fast asleep on the sofa. She didn't want to eat or drink anything, but I'm hungry and there are leftovers from last night's fish dinner: just enough for one. And *General Hospital* is good today. Sonny and Carly are at it again, and Jason's right in the middle of it all, as usual. That's one thing I love about the soaps: if you miss them for a day or a year they're easy to catch up with.

"Jayd, what am I doing in your house?" Misty asks as she slowly comes back to life. "And what's that foul smell?"

"Fish. Do you want some?" I must be in a good mood to offer this girl a bite of my food, especially red snapper and hush puppies. If Misty didn't look so weak I wouldn't offer her a damn thing.

"No. I don't have much of an appetite. And you didn't answer my question. What am I doing here?" I knew she would be ungrateful, but forgetful I wasn't expecting. I hope Mama found something to help Misty, because she's really freaking me out. I can't believe I'm thinking this way, but I want the old Misty back.

"I see someone's feeling better," Mama says, coming into the kitchen with what looks like a pitcher of lemonade. "Would you like something cold to drink, baby? It will make you feel better." At first I want to ask for a glass myself. However, the look on Mama's face tells me this drink—like the cats' breakfast—wasn't made for me.

"Thanks, Mrs. James," Misty says, accepting the tall glass Mama poured her. She drinks the cold potion down in three swift gulps. Mama promptly refills her glass for round two, smiling the entire time.

I can tell Mama's been up to more than juicing lemons by the way she's looking both at Misty and past her at Esmeralda's house. "I'm so sorry to hear about your grandmother," Mama says. Misty just nods her head and keeps drinking the lemonade like it's the best she's ever tasted. "So, how's your mom dealing with everything?"

"She's dealing," Misty says. "I should probably call her and let her know where I am," she says, nervously patting herself down, searching for her cell.

"It's in your purse," I say, passing her the heavy bag from the floor by the dining room table. Noticing the door open across the driveway, I look at Mama, who instinctively walks over to where I'm standing so she can see what I see: Esmeralda coming out onto her porch. Mama smiles a sinister grin, removes her apron and steps out onto the front porch.

"Thank you, Jayd," Misty says, taking her bag while I walk back to the front door to serve as a witness for the spiritual ass-whipping Esmeralda's about to get.

"Did I see Misty Truewell walk through your front door this morning?" Esmeralda says, almost whispering. Her cats surround her as if to serve as a force field to protect her from Mama's energy. I hope she knows by now that there's nothing that can protect her from my grandmother. Once she's got her eyes set on something, it's hers, good or bad. And, right now, Mama only has eyes for Esmeralda. "You know her people don't want you near that girl."

"What goes on in my house is my business. And I told you to mind yours a long time ago. You should've heeded my warning then," Mama says as she folds her arms across her chest, ready to fight. In her language, crossing your arms is tantamount to me taking my earrings off when it's time to get down. Before things can get real good, Misty joins us on the porch, purse and backpack in hand.

"My mom wants me to wait for her next door. Thank you for your hospitality," she says, almost pushing me out of her way as she practically runs across the way to our neighbor's house. Esmeralda opens the gate, letting Misty in, and promptly closes it behind her. She looks victorious, like she's just won the battle between her and Mama. But little does she know the war has only just begun. And Mama never loses.

"What was in that lemonade?" I ask her as I run my bath water before the rest of my uncles get home. Even with the short day at school it was still tiring, and I plan on turning in early tonight. By leaving at third period I missed the majority of my classes and drama rehearsal. But I did get my weekly assignments from English and I was able to finish the majority of them after Misty left a few hours ago.

"Water, lemons, and sugar, with a touch of honey," Mama says while filing her nails while standing in the bathroom doorway. I hope she gets some rest tonight and turns in even before I do.

"Well, how come I couldn't have any? I was thirsty too," I say, taking Mama's Esacada bubble bath and pouring it into my bath. I return the bottle to the medicine cabinet and she glares at me like I stole something.

"Because it wasn't for you. But there's plenty left in the refrigerator. Knock yourself out." I walk out of Mama's room and grab my toiletries and pajamas from Daddy's room, interrupting Jay and Bryan, obviously talking about something they don't want me to hear because they stop chatting as soon as I walk in. Who says dudes don't gossip? I walk back to Mama's room to finish our conversation before I soak my stress away in the tub.

"Come on, tell me what you gave to Misty," I say, wanting the full scoop.

"I just put some special honey in it to make her sweeter, so she wouldn't go off completely when she came to. You bringing her here wasn't the best idea, Jayd," Mama says, reaching across her bed to get a small vial of pink liquid from the shrine. "Put this in your bathwater. It'll help cleanse you from whatever's riding Misty." See, I knew she was up to something. I guess I can't be privy to everything Mama does. But I wish I could know more, for my own use. I still haven't been able to work on a remedy for Rah's problem, but I think Mama's got Misty's issues on lock.

"Well then, why did you let us come home?" I open the small bottle and take a whiff of the potion. It smells like cotton candy.

"Because of the urgency in your voice. Jayd, what you need to understand is that people have to desire our help for themselves. Misty's under Esmeralda's influence, which means there's nothing I can do for her unless she asks me to. Now yes, I could make a gris-gris for her or slip her a potion, but that would make me no better than Esmeralda, and that's not my style."

"But Misty doesn't know any better, and neither does her mom," I say, walking out of the bedroom and into the bathroom to turn off the bath water and empty the vial into it. It instantaneously fills the small room with its powerful aroma. "What's in this stuff?" I say, bringing the vial back to Mama, who's almost asleep.

"Good stuff. Now go soak and leave me alone, chile. I'm tired." I grab my shower cap from the dresser, ready for a relaxing bath. I know when Misty comes back to her true senses all hell is going to break loose. "And Jayd, it's admirable that you want to save the world. Actually, it's in your blood," she says, her emerald eyes quickly fading, but not before she gives me her final words of wisdom for the evening. "You can't save anyone but yourself, Jayd. Remember that and you'll avoid a lot of pain."

As I walk into the bathroom, I can't help but think about Misty and how KJ treated her today. I know Mama's usually right, but this time I think she may be a little wrong. I helped Jeremy without him knowing, and that worked out in his favor, even though we broke up. But still, the cupcakes got him out of going to jail. Misty and Rah both need some supernatural help to get out of their situations and I'm going to find a way to help them before the night is over. I guess I won't be turning in early after all.

After my bath, I creep into Mama's room to get the spirit book from behind the shrine. When she fed the Orishas and ancestors yesterday, she brought it into the house to look something up and forgot to put it back in the spirit room. Luckily Mama sleeps hard and I won't disturb her with my studies.

"Hey girl," I say to a snoozing Lexi as I step over her to enter the backhouse. I love being in here at night. It's so quiet and peaceful. I wish Mama would let me sleep out here, but that'll never happen. We still live in the hood and no matter how much spiritual protection we have around us, common sense should always prevail. It's already nine o'clock and I want to get to bed a little early. I spent all evening out here last night and a girl needs her beauty sleep.

I turn to Maman's section and look through her potions for getting rid of ill luck. I need something that'll work for both of them tomorrow. I wish I had time to personalize each

item I make. But, like Mama does with her clients, sometimes general is the best way to go.

"Unwebbed. I wonder what this is about," I say, as Lexi
settles into her position outside the screen door and makes
herself comfortable. She knows better than anyone that once
I set my mind to it, something's going to get made in this
room.

"It says that Maman made this gris-gris when her clients
got into situations that turned out the opposite of their ex-
pectations. It also says that the tiny satchel has to be placed
outside the backdoor of the person's home." Damn, that
means I'm going to have to go back over to Misty's house to
make sure this gris-gris takes effect. And I guess I'll have to
wait until this weekend to deliver Rah's. Maman also gives
specific instructions not to allow anyone to see where the
bag is concealed. How am I going to get this bag hidden in
Misty's yard without anyone noticing I'm there?

"Basil, honey, black peppercorns, three pennies and candy
for the crossroads. I wonder what that's for?" I read further
down, taking note of the remainder of the ingredients on the
list, as well as the chant that I need to say when I find a place
to put the charms. It's to Legba, the same Orisha Mama fed to
get rid of Esmeralda. I must be onto something here. All I
need is to find some fabric and string to tie up the ingredients in and to copy the chant down.

"This has got to work," I say, collecting the glass jars full of
herbs and other ingredients and placing them on the wooden
work table. I'll drop Misty's gris-gris off first thing in the
morning. I'll leave ten minutes early to make sure I can get in
and out without being noticed. Knowing Misty, she'll be running late. Hopefully I can get this done before she leaves. It
says here that it's important for the client to walk by the gris-
gris before they start their day, to ensure their luck is planted
firmly in their steps. I hope for Misty's sake it starts working

tomorrow. KJ's got her on tilt and I can't stand watching him humiliate her any longer. Besides, she can be my guinea pig before I try this out on Rah. If it reverses Misty's luck, even though she doesn't deserve it, then I know it will help Rah get away from Trish for good.

Rather than reset my regular alarm clock, I set my cell phone to wake me up early for this morning's adventure. I had to bury the bag in the yard overnight before planting it in Misty's yard, per Maman's final instructions. I can't wait to see if this charm bag will work. I hope nobody sees me, especially not Misty. If she found out that I was trying to help her like this, I'd never hear the end of it at school and around the neighborhood. And Mama would be completely pissed off.

"Jayd, why are you up so early?" Mama says groggily, not moving anything but her lips. I hate lying to Mama, but I can't tell her about this, not yet.

"I have some studying to do and I wanted to make sure I got in and out of the bathroom without any interference." Satisfied with my answer for now, she dozes back off to sleep. She must be really tired to let me get away from her inquisition that easy.

I get up and stumble in the dark as I feel my way around the foot of the bed. I retrieve my clothes for the day, which are hanging on the back of the door, and my toiletries inside my backpack, making for a quick exit to start my busy day. Too bad it has to start out by trying to help Misty. But here goes nothing.

I can't help but feel paranoid as I turn down Misty's block. The last time I was on Kemp, Felicia and her fellow hoodrats tried to jump me. It's barely six in the morning and not a soul is out this early around here. People are probably still in bed dreaming—good dreams, I hope. I, on the other hand, am speed walking down the dimly lit street, praying no loose dogs chase me or—even worse—blow my cover. I'm wearing my black Nike sweat suit with my hood pulled over my hair. I put my backpack under my jacket, just in case someone tries to identify me. The gris-gris is in my pocket and I'm ready to plant it and get on with the rest of my day.

When I reach Misty's yard, I look behind me to make sure the coast is clear and proceed to tiptoe toward the back. I see an empty planter behind the kitchen door. That'll be the perfect place to leave the small bag.

"Damn it," I whisper as a fat gray cat crosses my path, resting on the back porch. "I didn't know Misty had a cat," I say to myself as I walk up to the planter and lift it up, making sure the ground is dry—another prerequisite for planting the charm. Before I can leave it here, I have to say the chant one time and then walk backwards until I reach the curb, to make sure the bad luck doesn't follow me when I leave the house. As I reach in my other pocket for the index card with the words on it, I feel like someone's watching me.

"Legba, please don't confuse me. Let someone else be confused." Now that it's done, I can get out of here. This house has always given me the creeps. The slumbering cat, unaffected by my ritual, hasn't moved a muscle. But when it sees me walking backwards, it perks its head up and looks at me as if to ask, "What the hell are you doing?" Even the cat thinks I'm strange. I pull my cell phone out and check the time. I hope this works, for Misty's sake and for mine. South Bay High has enough drama without having to deal with KJ pimping Misty's ass on a daily basis. There's enough to deal with without having to be a part of *What's Love Got To Do With It?* the reality show.

* * *

"Good morning, sunshine," Chance says, ignoring my warnings, as usual, and hugging me as we continue to walk to class. The first bell rang a few minutes ago and I'm still hyped from this morning's good deed. My girls must be running late and I can't wait for them.

"What's up with you," I say, pulling away from him slightly. I'm getting a different vibe from him and it's making me uncomfortable. "When are you going to get it through that thick skull of yours that you can't flirt with me like you used to do before you started dating Nellie?" I say, pushing him in the shoulder. "You're spoken for now, remember?"

"Yeah, yeah. But I can still give my homegirl a friendly hug, can't I?" Chance puts his right arm around my shoulders, pulling me in close.

"Stop it, Chance," I say, trying to squirm my way out of his arms, but he's got me on lock. "I don't want to smell like you." Even if he does smell good, I prefer my Egyptian Musk oil to his Polo cologne any day.

"Okay, I get the hint. So, how do you like the rehearsals so far?" he says as I step into my Spanish class. I'm disappointed to see Mr. Donald's here today. I wonder when Mr. Adewale will start on a permanent basis. As many sick days as our regular teacher takes, I'm sure he'll be back soon.

"It's okay. I wish we didn't have to share our class with ASB. It's already cramped enough in there as it is." I notice Mickey, Nigel, and Nellie rushing across campus to their class. They don't even notice Chance and me talking, they're in such a hurry.

"There's the bell, girl," Chance says, giving me a final hug good-bye. "I've got to go." All of the students on the late boat with my friend are rushing to get to class before the bell stops ringing. The only thing I'm concerned with today is whether or not Misty acts any different. After she drank Mama's lemonade yesterday she looked much better, but not back to the Misty we know and hate. Who knows what happened to her after she went over to Esmeralda's house yesterday? I never saw her mom come for her and she wasn't on the bus this morning.

Before I can turn around to go to my seat, in the distance I notice Misty following KJ. I guess she's back to rolling with him after all. Maybe that's a good sign that the gris-gris is working. I'll have to wait until lunch to see for myself. If she's still walking around like a zombie, I know it hasn't taken yet. I'm not too sure how quickly her luck will turn around. But knowing Maman's work, it won't take long.

Because I missed the majority of the school day yesterday, I had some catching up to do in government and math. Jeremy missed me yesterday, but tried to play it off like he was about to give away my seat, which was really cute. I'm glad we're able to maintain a civil friendship amid the hurt of our breakup. I wonder if he's dating someone new already.

"Hey, Jayd. What happened to you yesterday?" Mickey says, walking up to our usual bench with her lunch tray packed. "You disappeared after you went to bat for Misty. I thought KJ kidnapped you or something."

"Are you going to eat all of that by yourself?" Nigel asks, walking up with Chance and Jeremy in tow. What's Jeremy doing here at lunch? Usually he's off-campus and I know he and Nigel aren't that cool.

"What I eat is none of your business. I told you not to come near me unless you had a new BlackBerry with you," Mickey says, biting into her cheeseburger before stuffing her face with fries. She has a large Coke and chocolate ice cream to wash it all down with. I know my girl can eat, but this is an unusually large lunch, even for Mickey. "And what are you

doing here anyway?" Mickey says, looking straight at Jeremy.
I'd like to know myself.

"Me and Chance have some business to take care of. Care
to join us?" Jeremy says, looking at me as I peel the banana
that I brought from home. I also packed a pear and some
crackers, along with my bottled water. I'm trying to save all of
my cash, especially since I didn't work too many hours this
weekend and that means no more buying lunch until I'm
sure about my income flow. Unfortunately, my hours are still
cut until further notice, really messing up my timeline for
buying my car.

"I'm cool. Shouldn't you be in the drama room? I thought
today's lunch rehearsal was a fitting for the dudes' costumes,"
I say, biting into my fruit, envious of Mickey's meal. "And,
where's Nellie?"

"Nellie's running late. She had to retake an English quiz
from yesterday. Nellie needs to get on her schoolwork in a
real way," Chance says, looking across the quad toward
South Central where KJ, his boys, and the rest of South Central are hanging out. Misty seems a little better, but she still
looks like a zombie to me. "What did you ever see in him?"
Chance says. Jeremy's eyes follow mine and then he looks
dead at me, making the heat in my body rise to my cheeks.

"I don't know," I say, taken aback by my still apparent feelings for Jeremy, who hasn't taken his eyes off me yet. He
looks extra yummy today, in his khaki shorts and blue Polo
shirt that sets off his eyes. He decided to let his bushy curls
run wild today, instead of trapping them all up in a hat. I bet
if I hugged Jeremy his smell would rub off on me. But unlike
with Chance, I don't think I'd mind.

"Same thing we always see in these fools; nothing," Mickey
says to Nigel as Jeremy and I break our connection and re-
join the conversation. Nigel looks like he wants to slap Mickey

in the face. Lucky for us all he doesn't believe in hitting women.

"Jayd, will you check your girl, please," Nigel says, looking for some love. But I'm with her on this one.

"I can't say she's entirely wrong. We do see what we want to see when it comes to our men," I say, telling the truth. Jeremy looks slightly disappointed in my response, but still amused. "And usually, the trick's on us. We end up getting hurt and cleaning up the aftermath while the dudes are free to explore new terrain."

"Not always," Jeremy says, walking over to sit next to me on the bench. My heart's fluttering fast, like the first time we talked at Matt's house. Why can't relationships stay that blissful indefinitely? "Sometimes it's the girl who tricks the guy and rebounds into someone else's arms, even if she knows that she's not over the first dude." Mickey, Nigel, and Chance are all speechless, noticing the vibe has shifted. Nigel looks at me, completely annoyed, as Nellie walks up, again shifting my world off its axis. And this time I'm thankful for the intrusion.

"Hey, did I miss anything?" Nellie says, taking Chance's Snapple from his hand and taking a swig.

"I've got work to catch up on. I'll check y'all later," I say, hugging Nellie before taking off down the hill. Jeremy rises from his seat next to me, ready to walk me down.

"Where are you rushing off to? I just got here," she says, looking as confused as I suddenly feel.

"I need to catch up on yesterday's work," I say. I never told anyone that I took Misty back to my house. And, knowing her, she didn't either. I hope it stays our little secret.

"Want an escort?" Jeremy says, causing Nigel to glare at me even harder. The last thing I need is more bull from Jeremy. I admit, we never said we weren't attracted to each other. And, yes, I'm still feeling him. But I have no respect for the way he lives his life and I can't stand his family values. There's no hope for us as far as I'm concerned, even if I am still rocking my Lucky bag and the gold "J" bracelet he gave me. What can I say; Jeremy has good taste. He has to in order to buy his way out of all the bullshit he can put a girl through.

"No, I think I'll walk alone for now." And until I can sort out my feelings, I think it should stay that way. However, that doesn't change my plans for helping Rah. It's bigger than us being able to get back together. Having Trish completely out of the picture is a must no matter what happens to us. And from the looks of Misty's smiling face, I'm the girl for the job, no matter how I get it done.

~ 13 ~
What the Hell?

"She's hot, she's danger/
Everybody knows her name yeah."

—T.O.K./PITBULL

After yesterday's emergency rescue with Misty, Mama and Netta have been talking about nothing else ever since. I'm scared to tell them about the gris-gris I made for Misty and the one I'm planning on making for Rah. But Mama was grateful I made the eye patch to help her sleep and I didn't ask her permission for that. Maybe she won't be too upset that I tried to help Misty without her knowing about it. After all, it's the thought that counts, right?

"Jayd, hand me that towel, please," Netta says, ringing the water out of Mama's hair. "I think it's honorable that you want to help that girl out, especially after all the shit she's put you through in the name of friendship," Netta says, squeezing Mama's head tightly. "Besides, Jayd, your Mama has been guilty of helping folks who didn't ask for it back in her day too."

"Yes, and we both know how those situations turned out, don't we, Netta," Mama says as Netta sits her straight up in her chair at the washbasin to finish towel-drying her hair. Next comes Netta's leave-in conditioner that Mama helped her create. If they would get a patent for their hair products we'd all be millionaires. But for some reason, they refuse to sell the recipes. "Don't encourage the girl, Netta. And watch your heavy hands on my head," she says as Netta continues to squeeze her head, pulling her eyes tightly.

"Oh hush up, Lynn Mae," Netta says, smearing Mama's jet-black hair with the tropical-scented cream. I think they put a mixture of mango, pineapple and avocado in this one. The natural ingredients are what make it smell so good. The aroma's also making me hungry since I barely had a chance to eat today. It was my first rehearsal playing opposite Reid, and it took a lot out of me, making me lose my appetite in the process. Reid is very convincing in his role as the twisted king: a part he was born to play.

"Hush up nothing, Netta. If Jayd can avoid the madness that comes with trying to help ungrateful people, then why shouldn't she?" I know Mama's trying to protect me, but I've got this one under control. She doesn't know about my mystic cupcakes that helped Jeremy out of his possible incarceration, and that worked out fine. She just needs more faith in my abilities and I'm going to prove to her that I'm ready to take the next step in my legacy.

"Who says they'll be ungrateful?" I'm glad Netta's here to fight my battles for me. I can't see how my mom didn't like her when she was growing up. I don't know what I'd do without her and our Tuesdays at the shop. It's like she says everything I want to say to Mama but can't because she's my elder. And I've learned not to question her too much if I want to keep all of my teeth. But Netta's her homegirl and equal, making it an even playing field.

"Experience, that's who. And you know better than anyone how evil ungrateful people can be, especially when they don't understand how we work." Looking from me to Mama, Netta notices how quiet I am, calling Mama's attention to it as well. I can't hide anything from them for too long, but I'm not ready to tell them about this morning's adventures at Misty's.

"Jayd, why are you so quiet? Everything okay?" Netta asks, walking Mama over to her station to blow-dry her hair. I think Mama's going for cornrows today. She's been complaining about her head itching in her French roll all week and, like me, braids are her alternate style.

"Yes, everything's fine. Just worried about Misty, that's all," I say without completely blowing my cover, or so I think. Mama's eyes tell me she knows I'm up to something; even if she doesn't know what it is yet.

"That girl needs all the help she can get, especially now," Netta says. I think she can feel me plotting too, and wants to come to my defense. Mama, on the other hand, isn't so sympathetic. Netta drapes Mama with a pretty pink-and-yellow hair cape before sitting on her stool, ready to work Mama's do. I love to watch Netta make magic on Mama's head. I wonder if she wants an apprentice. I would love to work here.

"Rule number one Jayd, you must have your clients' permission before you can do any work on their behalf. To do otherwise is being dishonest and that's not how we do it in our house," she shouts over the loud blow-dryer Netta's combing though her shoulder-length hair. "That's why I asked the cats' permission to use their sight. I respect individuals' souls, girl, even animals'," Mama says, lowering her chin to allow Netta to dry the back of her head.

"How did you ask the cats, Mama?" I say from my seat in the adjacent station. I don't understand why Netta has two stations when she's the only stylist in the shop. She has the same steady clientele—no walk-ins allowed, unlike the other shops around here that'll take anyone off the street. Doing hair up in here means more than the average press and curl. When a client leaves Netta's shop, she leaves with a flyy hairstyle and blessings, too.

"I knew Esmeralda wouldn't give me the time of day, so I went to the next best resource, her pets. When I made them breakfast, Jayd, that was my way of giving them an offering to request the use of their vision. First I offered them the milk, which had my special honey blend to sweeten them up." I wonder if it's the same honey she gave to Misty? If so, I hope its effect never wears off. School would be much nicer if Misty wouldn't trip as often.

"Your Mama's good with that honey, chile," Netta says, shutting the dryer off and brushing through Mama's hair, ready to style it. "Nobody can sweeten a tongue like Queen Jade, a.k.a. Lynn Mae Williams."

"Then I gave them the cupcakes with a little something extra in them to help facilitate the exchange. You see, Jayd, I didn't deceive or manipulate anyone. And Esmeralda can be as mad as she wants but I didn't break any rules in what I did. The interaction was between me and her fur balls, not her—and it was mutually beneficial."

"But what if your target doesn't have any pets?" Which is the case with Rah. I didn't know Misty had adopted a cat. As a matter of fact, I remember her being allergic to animal fur. But maybe that's changed over the years or perhaps it was just a stray looking for a place to rest.

"There are many ways to influence a situation without directly hitting your target. That's what your studies are for, Jayd. Don't put the cart before the horse," she says, dropping her old-school wisdom on me as Netta parts her scalp for braids. "What you need is one of Netta's head cleansings, girl. You know better than to let these people mess with your emotions. You've got better things to do anyway."

"Oh Jayd, you'll love it, girl," Netta says, leaving Mama's head to escort me over to the wash basin Mama just left. "I'll finish your braids in a minute, Lynn Mae," she says, too excited to get her hands in my head. "I haven't touched your crown since you were about nine days old. Look at all of this hair," she says, releasing my hair from the tight ponytail and rubbing her fingers across my scalp. Damn, her touch feels good.

"Yes, at your naming ceremony," Mama says, smiling as she recalls the event. I can remember a little bit of it, but it all comes flooding back as Netta runs the cool water over my hair. "Your mom had a fit when she found out I let Netta touch your head."

"Yeah, Lynn Marie hasn't liked me too much ever since I caught her making out in the backhouse when she was fifteen years old and I told your grandmother on her," Netta says, but I'm too relaxed to keep up with the conversation. This feels so good. I wish I could let people in my head all the time, but Mama says it's a serious taboo for me. Only when she's around and only people she trusts can touch my head.

"Jayd, after Netta does this, you're going to need to wear white for the next twenty-four hours," Mama says, going into Netta's closet and grabbing two long white cloths to wrap my head up in. I already feel much better. But I don't know about wearing all white to school.

"I'm going to stick out like a sore thumb if I come to school in nothing but white clothes." It's bad enough I don't fit in already. If I go to school looking like I was just baptized, they'll really have something to say.

"You already stick out, Jayd. Don't worry about what others think of you. Be proud of your lineage, girl, even if it means you have to stand up for yourself at school. Know that what's in you is much stronger than anything that's in the world." And I know she's right. I just hope Misty and Rah feel the same way and trust that I would never do anything to hurt them. I know Rah will always give me the benefit of the doubt, but Misty is another story.

* * *

I see Misty coming at me with a torch, shouting "Witch, witch!" My jade bracelets fall off my arm to the ground, shattering my powers along with their fragile forms.

"You don't have the sight, child," the evil woman's voice says. "And you never will!"

"Yes I do!" I shout at the veiled voice as I look down through my tears at the shattered bracelets Mama entrusted to me. Misty and her followers are on a serious witch hunt and I'm the only one standing accused, which means I should be running for my life.

"Just admit it. Those pretty brown eyes are no good without your bracelets," the voice hisses. "The legacy ends right here, right now. Give it up, Jayd, before you get hurt."

"My eyes are just as good as my mother's and my grandmother's, not to mention my ancestors," I shout. But the longer I stand here fighting with this unseen voice, the closer Misty and haters get to burning my ass alive. I've already been scorched in one dream and this isn't about to be round two.

"She's learning the hard way, but she's still learning," Mama's voice says. She, like the other woman, is nowhere to be seen. "Move out of the way when you see fire coming toward you, Jayd. Otherwise, you will get burned." I touch the scar on my arm, remembering the painful incident, and decide it's time to face my fears.

"Witch, witch," Misty shouts louder, egging on the crowd. "Get her!" As the crowd comes toward me at full speed, I recognize some of the faces as my own friends. Mickey and Nellie are on the front line right beside Misty, ready to light me like a Christmas tree.

"I knew you were weird, Jayd, but damn. I didn't know you were a witch," Mickey says, sucking on her Blow Pop while lighting a torch of her own.

"Yeah, Jayd. That's really something you need to tell

folks. I mean, what would the people at my church think of me if they knew I was hanging out with a witch," Nellie says, putting her torch to Mickey's to light it, too. Before I can run off, I'm trapped in place and suddenly tied to a makeshift stake, like so many gifted conjure women before me.

"Mama, help!" I yell. But all I can hear are the chants of the angry crowd surrounding me. Before they can get the roast started, Rah runs up to the crowd carrying a water hose and puts out everyone's torches, saving my ass.

"I'm a survivor." My phone rings, waking me from my nightmare just in the nick of time. When I fold back the comforter, I realize I'm dripping in a pool of sweat. My sheets are cold and my white T-shirt is clinging to my body. If Mama saw me like this she'd have a fit. I learned at an early age never to be too revealing in a house full of men, even if they're related to you. And Mama will never let me forget it either. What's Rah doing calling me so early? Something must be wrong.

"Hello," I say, out of breath. I feel like I just ran ten miles and I don't run unless a dog's chasing me.

"Jayd, are you okay?" he says, sounding short of breath too. "I just had the weirdest dream about you." Oh hell no. Not him too.

"Yes, I'm fine," I say, sitting up in bed and reaching over to the nightstand for my alarm clock. It would have rung in five minutes anyway. No need for it now because I'm wide awake. "What was your dream about?" I whisper into the phone as I creep out of my bed and grab my daily necessities. I don't want to wake Mama up. I'll tell her about this one later, after I get Rah's side of the story too.

"It was about you running from the law or some shit. It could've been about me, but I felt like you were the one in trouble." Rah has never called me about a dream like this before. "Are you sure you're okay?" He sounds very concerned and I think it's about more than his dream.

"What else is going on?" I ask, dashing through the cold hall and into the dark bathroom, closing the door behind me. I quickly plug the electric heater into the wall and sit on the toilet seat directly in front of it, waiting for the orange glow to appear and warm my damp body.

"I think you may have been right about Trish," he says, giving me the full confession. "She told her brother that I got another girl, and he's not feeling his sister being unhappy, know what I mean?"

"Yeah, I know," I say, propping the phone against my shoulder and hugging myself to get more warmth. I hate cold mornings. "Well, I'll be honest too," I say, stretching my hands out to nearly touch the small heater with my fingertips. "I've been working on something to help you get away from Trish." Unlike with Misty, I'm going to be honest in my approach with him. Rah's my real friend and deserves to know the truth about my efforts.

"Something like what, Jayd?" he says. I can tell from his tone that he's already not feeling me. But he seems willing to listen and that's a good start.

"Well, you know Mama makes charms to help influence people's destinies, right?" I say, realizing that I'm not making this sound very good. Now I see why Mama said we must have a client's permission or request to do work on his or her behalf. If you don't, the conversation starts off like this one.

"Right. What does that have to do with me? I didn't ask her for anything," he says.

"I know, baby. But I did some work on your behalf, or I was planning on it, that is, if you don't mind. Do you mind?"

I ask, sounding like the twelve-year-old girl he fell in love with.

"Hell yeah I mind, Jayd," he says, yelling into the phone. I didn't think he'd be this upset. But he is and it's all my fault. "What were you thinking?"

"I was thinking I would try to help your ass get out of this mess with Trish. Forgive me for caring," I say. Even if he is right, his attitude puts me on the defense.

"I don't mind you wanting to help, Jayd. What I mind is you doing some shit behind my back. And who gave you permission to wear your grandmother's apron?" he says, referring to Mama's crown as queen of the kitchen—special recipes included. "Does she know you're going around putting spells on people and shit?"

"You're taking this a little too far, don't you think?" I say. "You have a right to be mad, but don't get crazy with it."

"Jayd, this is serious. I don't want to start having dreams and getting headaches and shit like you do. That scares the hell out of me, girl, on the real," he says. And for the first time, I get it. Rah accepts my spiritual lineage just as much as any outsider of the religion can. But he's as afraid of it as anyone else, too.

"I'm sorry. I didn't mean to scare you," I say, eyeing my things sitting on the overfilled clothes hamper. It always smells like feet and ass in here. "I can't stand to see people hurting, Rah, you included. If I can do something within my powers to help, I will. But you're right. I should've never done it without your permission," I say. His silence worries me, but I'm not hanging up until I know we're okay. As my dream predicted, Rah is my one true ally in our circle who will always be there for me, no matter what. And I can't afford to lose him now, even if that means having to deal with Trish in his life for a little while longer.

"What were you going to do?" he says, sounding more curious than angry.

"I was making you a gris-gris similar to the one hanging on my backpack with the word 'listen' written on the side."

"Are you sure you don't have some dolls with pins sticking out of them or some shit like that?" Rah says, making light of our heritage. But it's okay. I think he'll learn to be more comfortable with it in time.

"No, not this time. Just a little herb sack, if you will." I hear the door to my grandfather's room open and know I've woken someone up. I better get off this phone and get ready for school before that someone knocks on the door.

"There's never anything wrong with an herb sack," he says, easing up a bit. I'm glad he wasn't unappeasable on the subject. He must really trust me to forgive me so quickly for invading his privacy. "For real though, Jayd. Baby, I know you've got skills that the rest of us don't have. And everyone knows that Mama is nice with her talents too," he says. I love that he has so much affection for Mama. "But you can't pull nothing like this again. I need to have a choice in the matter, always, understand?"

"I hear you, Rah I hear you." Before we hang up, I turn on the shower to let it run for a while. Sometimes it can take up to five minutes for the hot water to work. "So, do I have your permission?" I say, not giving up on my mission. What kind of queen in training would I be if I retreated at the first sign of trouble?

"It can't be too frightening if it's herb bags, I guess," he says, bending to my will. I guess that sweetness lesson is finally kicking in, too. "But I want to see you make it," he says.

"No problem. You know you're the only friend of mine Mama will let in her backhouse." She's very finicky about who she lets into the spirit room, clients included. "I won't make a move without your consent, I promise. Talk to you later."

"All right then. And Jayd, thanks for telling me the truth," he says, hanging up on the conversation. I'm glad we got that out, but it still doesn't explain why he had a dream about me running while I was having a similar one. That'll be first on my agenda when I talk to Mama this afternoon. I still have to get through school first and I better go if I want to get there on time.

"Jayd, get out of the bathroom. I hear you in there talking on the phone. I gotta go, now girl. Come on," Jay says, interrupting my flow.

"You'll have to wait until I'm out of the shower," I say, stepping into the steaming water and officially starting my day. There's nothing like a nice hot shower to make me feel good first thing in the morning.

"Whatever. I'll go outside," he says, going out into the cold morning to handle his business and leaving me to mine. I'm glad Rah and I were able to resolve our issue instead of letting it fester until it was out of control. I'm also grateful he gave me permission to help him, although I hope there are no repercussions from making Misty's bag without her knowledge. Even if there are, it'll be worth it as long as she gets her mojo back. The gris-gris Netta gave me is sitting on the shrine until Mama finishes her work. I will pay closer attention to Misty today to see if I can tell any difference in her spirit.

It was an unusually quiet bus ride this morning. Now that Misty seems to be back in her routine with KJ, she's no longer on the bus, invading what I consider to be my space, especially when she's at my stop in the morning. It's enough having to see her at school all day. I don't need to see her first thing in the morning.

Instead of speeding up the hill to campus like I normally do every morning, I decide to take it slow and enjoy the view of nicely manicured lawns and dream about having a luxury car like the various ones parked in the driveways of the mini mansions I stroll by. What's the rush? I don't want to catch up on the gossip nor do I want to run into any of my friends. After last night's dream and Rah's call this morning, I'm in need of some serious me time.

"Hey Jayd. Can I holla at you for a minute?" Jeremy says, pulling up next to me and ruining my silent vibe. "Get in."

"I'm flying solo this morning, Jeremy, but thank you for the offer," I say, not changing my steady pace. My legs are used to the walk now and it's not as much of a challenge for me anymore. It actually feels good, and I see the muscles building in my thighs. If I could afford it, I'd get a new skirt or two and show them off.

"Come on," he says, cruising alongside me while the other cars angrily pass him. "You're stopping traffic, Lady J."

"No, you're stopping traffic. I'm walking to school," I say, not giving in to his charming smile. "Shouldn't you be surfing or something?"

"Come on, girl. Why are you being so difficult? I just want to talk, see how you're doing." Why am I giving him such a hard time? I really can't answer that, but I know it has a lot to do with Rah. My mom used to say two men cannot occupy the same space at the same time, especially if one of them is a black man, and I know she's right. After what happened between Mickey and Nigel on Friday, I never want to go out with two dudes at the same time again.

"Jeremy, we can catch up in class," I say, trying to brush him off gently. But he's not taking the hint. He finally pulls over and gets out of his car, really pissing off the other students driving toward campus. It's a tight street and there's no room for cars parked on the side. "What are you doing?" I say, stopping short as he steps in front of me.

"Look, Jayd, I made a mistake. A huge, terrible mistake and I want us to try again," he says. I admit, I have daydreamed of this moment, but I never thought it would actually come true, especially not like this. Too bad this type of thing only works in the movies.

"Jeremy," I say, reacting slowly to his revelation. I don't want to argue with him and I'm not telling him about Rah either. "Have you conveniently forgotten that your family's a tad bit on the racist side?" I say, folding my arms across my chest and looking him straight in the eyes. He towers over me, and I have to stretch my neck up to look at him.

"Not me, Jayd. I'm not racist and I'm the only one you need to worry about from now on. Jayd, I meant it when I said that I love you. Why can't we start over?"

"Because we're too different and our family values are on opposite sides of existence, that's why." I step past him and try to continue my trek, but Jeremy takes hold of my hand and spins me around to face him. Why is he making this so difficult?

"We don't have to let our families separate us, Jayd. Come on. We had a good thing going before all of that mess with Tania started," he says, ignoring the facts completely. It's convenient for him to live in his own reality. I, on the other hand, have to live in the real world and dating a man whose family doesn't like strong black women, like the women I come from and the woman I am growing into, won't cut it.

"No, Jeremy. It started when your dad decided that black women were to be seen and not heard, screwed but not reproduced with." Jeremy, looking overwhelmed but not defeated, holds my hand even tighter before bringing it up to his lips for a gentle kiss.

"I'm not giving up on you. Never," he says, playing with the heavy gold bangle hanging from my wrist.

"What if I told you that you got out of jail partially because

of something I did?" I say, ready to test out this whole honesty philosophy on Jeremy. If he really loves me, he'll accept
my beliefs whether he believes in God or not.

"What do you mean? Are you talking about your prayers or
something like that?" he says, already mocking my faith.

"Something like that," I say, going for the full confession.
"Remember the cupcakes I made for you the day before your
hearing?" I say, reliving our first kiss, which came after he devoured the tasty treats.

"Yeah. Those were the best-tasting cupcakes I've ever had.
But don't tell my mom," he says, making light of the situation. I hope he finds the humor in what I'm about to reveal.

"They were more than good, Jeremy. They were, shall we
say, very special cupcakes with a little something in them to
help you get out of going to jail." Looking at me in disbelief,
Jeremy laughs hysterically, unable to control himself.

"Are you serious?" he says. "You really think that you baked
a dessert that could help the charges against me get dropped?
If that's the case, then why did we hire a lawyer?" Watching
him get a kick out of my admission, I pull away from him and
continue my stride.

"Never mind I said anything. I knew you wouldn't understand," I say as the first bell rings. Now I'm going to be late
and our little talk wasn't even worth it. I'm glad Rah was
more receptive than Jeremy. How can he make jokes about
something so serious to me? Mama's right, some people are
ungrateful no matter what you do for them. Good intentions
definitely pave the road to hell and, after my last dream, I
have a feeling I'm on my way there now.

~ 14 ~
Devil in a White Tee

"Don't ask my neighbors, come to me/
Don't be afraid of what you see."

—THE EMOTIONS

When I finally reach the main hall, I see a crowd of folks in the attendance office. I wonder what's going on? But I don't have time to be nosey and I don't want anyone noticing my all-white ensemble yet. Maybe it won't seem so strange. After all, I did wear all black yesterday, right down to my boots. I've got less than two minutes to get to first period and I need to stop by my locker first to get my books. I guess me being late is better than showing up on time without my materials.

"Jayd," Nigel says from the double doors leading into the main hall. "I have to talk to you."

"Not now, Nigel. I've got to get to class." The hall's almost empty, except for Misty and her crew at my locker. And, by the look of it, they're not there to help me carry my books. Oh shit, she knows. How did she find out?

"Jayd, listen to me," Nigel says, falling into step with me as I charge toward my fate. Mama told me to be strong in who I am and that's just what I'm going to do. "Misty's been waiting for you all morning. She's started some sort of witch hunt against you and you need to come with me now, Jayd. Rah's on his way to get you as we speak. Don't worry about the absence; I'll get Mr. Donald to cover for us. Jayd, did you hear a word I just said?"

"Yes, Nigel, and I already know what's going on," I say, stopping to face my friend. Nigel's known me for longer than any of these people up here and even his fear has gotten the best of him. "Do you believe that I'm a witch?" I don't know what Rah's told him, but I know he's had his suspicions about my dreams and my grandmother since junior high.

"It doesn't matter what I believe, Jayd. This isn't about me," he says, avoiding the question. But I want to know his answer.

"You're not going to hurt my feelings, Nigel. Just tell me the truth. Do you believe I'm a witch?"

"No, girl, of course not. But, y'all do be doing some strange stuff up in that house of yours," he says, looking me up and down. "And why are you wearing all white? Still want to be nurse Coffy?" he says, making fun of my Halloween costume. Before I can offer him an explanation, Misty looks in my direction and points me out to her crowd.

"There she is!" Misty marches toward me with KJ, Shae, and the rest of South Central right behind her. Just as my dream predicted, they look hungry for blood, and mine is the only type on the menu. Nellie and Mickey enter from the side entrance, watching the procession of angry students head my way. They look confused, like they want to help but are unsure of what to do.

"Jayd, let's go back in the main hall," Nigel says, grabbing my arm and trying to pull me away. But I'm not afraid of them at all, especially not Misty. Her family's just as involved in voodoo as mine, and she's got no right to throw stones at me.

"Nigel, what do you think is going to happen to me?" I say, pulling my arm from his hand, as Misty gets closer. Nellie and Mickey try to walk ahead of them, but Misty's on a mission and she won't let anyone get in her way.

"Jayd, you're not invincible, no matter what you think." As Misty advances, she throws the gris-gris at me, hitting me in the face. That didn't feel good, but at least it's not a flaming torch trying to barbeque my ass.

"Damn," Del says. Those are my sentiments exactly. I wasn't expecting her to throw the bag at me. How did she find it? I know she's not into planting or any other outdoor activity.

"What the hell are you doing snooping around my house, Jayd?" Misty says, stepping up to me like she's going to hit me. But I know her better than that. She's all bark and no bite, even though she has a good arm. The bag did hurt a little when it hit my cheek, but that was a lucky toss.

"I was just trying to help," I say, starting off with the truth. The final bell rings above our heads, but no one moves.

"Help, my ass. That's why you kidnapped me from school on Monday, so you could get my DNA and put it in this bag. You buried it; that means you wanted me buried so you could have KJ all to yourself," she says. Now she's really not making any sense.

"Misty, you've been in my house before and I see you at school every day. If I wanted your DNA I could have gotten it in many other ways." As soon as the words leave my mouth I realize they don't help my case much. Mickey and Nellie even look shocked at my confession, as the crowd circles around Misty and me, anticipating a fight. "And for the record, I didn't kidnap you. I saved your ass from KJ's harassment."

"He wasn't harassing me, Jayd, and I don't remember asking for your help," she says, KJ right behind her. I bet he loves this. "Thank God the cat dug up the bag and gave it to me when I got home yesterday. Otherwise, who knows where I'd be."

"You don't remember shit, Misty. That was part of your problem. Like I said, I wanted to help. But now I know better," I say. This broad's really got her nerve coming at me like this. "And I know you're not stupid enough to think that I want KJ's trifling ass back."

"Don't call my man trifling," she says, putting her hands on her wide hips and getting as far up in my face as she can. I look down at her, waiting for her next move. "You're just mad because both of your relationships ended quickly because you're weird. I told you that before and I'll say it again. You and your grandmother are witches and now I have proof," she says, picking up the charm bag from the ground and displaying it again for everyone to see.

"Misty, you don't know what you're talking about. That bag was to help you keep your house before you get thrown out on the street, or was that supposed to be a secret?" I say, letting her business out. "I know all about your grandmother and the house and your mama and Esmeralda, too. Who, by the way, is the real witch if there ever was one," I say, causing the mob to look around in disbelief.

"You're lying," Misty says, tossing the bag back down on the ground in front of me. This can't be good for her luck. "My mom wouldn't have anything to do with Esmeralda if she was a witch. You and your family are the evil ones on the block, sneaking around people's houses in the dark."

"I'm sure whatever Jayd did was for a good reason," Nigel says, stepping in between me and Misty.

"I agree," Jeremy says, entering the hall. He must've just got here, but I don't know why it took him so long to get up the hill. Maybe he had some business to take care of. I hope it was legal, because I'm not doing anymore work for anyone for a very long time. Rah will be my last client until I'm ready to deal with the heat that comes along with wearing this crown.

"Well, I don't," KJ says, restoring the negative energy in the large space. "I knew something was strange about you when we were dating, but I couldn't put my finger on it. Now it all makes sense," he says. I knew if he ever got the chance to kick me when I was down he would. That's the kind of punk he is.

"Don't call my girl strange," Rah says, stepping up behind me, sandwiching me between him and Nigel. "You need to back off before you get hurt." Jeremy looks completely taken aback as Rah claims his territory, which isn't officially his to declare. But now is not the time for that argument. "Jayd, let's go," Rah says. And, with Rah and Nigel leading the way, I decide not to fight and follow them out of this mess.

Thank goodness I had AP meetings all day, as well as rehearsal. Mrs. Bennett chose our next book to study for the AP exam, which is the play *The Crucible*. Ironically, there's a female slave in it who is accused of being a witch. When I asked more about her, Mrs. Bennett's ears perked up like satellite dishes. She's always up in the students' business. I wonder if she's already heard about Misty's accusations against me?

I was glad to be away from the masses today, protected by my club allegiances. Misty's made it seem like I'm stalking her. That's the furthest thing from the truth and I know she knows better. I'll have to give Mama the full scoop when I get home, which means I'll also have to brace myself for her wrath. And I thought I was in trouble here! Misty's tantrum is nothing compared to what Mama's going to do to me when she finds out I went against her rules.

The bus ride home was more tense than usual. I found myself looking over my shoulder at each stop, waiting for Misty to jump out and confront me on the street, but it never happened. I even half-expected Felicia and her crew to be waiting for me at the stop by Miracle Market, but all was clear for my walk home. No matter how many different ways I try to phrase it in my head, me making a gris-gris for Misty with-

out her permission doesn't sound right to me, which means
Mama won't buy it either. I better get it straight in my head
before I tell Mama. I want her to be on my side, and that's
not going to happen if I don't sound sincere in acknowledg-
ing my mistake.

"Hi Mama," I say, walking in the backdoor and entering
the kitchen. It smells good in here. Mama's making baked
chicken, rice, cornbread and greens: one of my favorite din-
ners.

"Hi baby," she says as I kiss her cheek before I put my bag
down on the floor and wash my hands in the kitchen sink.
"How was school?" she says, sifting the cornmeal and flour
into the mixing bowl. I take the eggs and buttermilk out of
the refrigerator and put them on the table, ready to help finish preparing the feast. Jay is in his room doing God knows
what and my uncles aren't home yet. Daddy has bible study
tonight, so he probably won't be home until later. Mama and
Daddy still aren't talking after his latest fan dropped by, so I
doubt any of this food is for him anyway.

"School was okay," I say, not ready to talk about Misty yet.
I want to get in the house good and settle down before I
bring up the unpleasant subject to Mama. "How were things
at home?" It's almost time for the holidays, another busy season for Mama's clientele. People are always looking for good
luck charms to bring them money and lovers during the
Christmas season.

"Very interesting, actually," Mama says, cracking two eggs
into the batter. She looks at the yolks' formation and then
looks at me. I can tell by her eyes that she already knows
what I've done. "Misty and her mom came by to visit Esmeralda
today. You wouldn't happen to know anything about that,
would you?" Mama says, holding the glass bowl with one
hand and mixing the cornbread batter with the other. I knew

she would find out, but I didn't know Misty would be the one to tell.

"Mama, I was going to tell you about the gris-gris today," I say, trying to defuse the situation. But Mama's vigorous beating tells me she's not in the mood.

"Jayd, I've told you a million times about dealing with Misty. And it's not enough that you already know that Esmeralda's a dangerous woman, but Misty has a connection to her and you still disobeyed me. What's gotten into you, girl?"

"I was just trying to help," I say, sounding like a five-year-old child. I hate it when Mama gets mad at me. I feel bad for working her nerves.

"I haven't died and made you queen yet, Jayd," Mama says, stopping me in my tracks. The tears well up in my eyes as Mama glares down at me, never missing a beat with her batter. "I'm the one who makes the decisions about how our work is spread and to whom, not you. You deliberately went against the rules, Jayd, and that sounds too much like Lynn Marie for me."

"I'm sorry, Mama," I say. She sounds hurt in more ways than one. "I'm so sorry."

"I know you are. Look at you. You look worn out, girl. That's what happens when you do the devil's work," Mama says, pouring the mixture into the hot cast iron skillet glazed with butter. "You need to eat a good dinner and go to bed. No more sneaking out in the morning to put bags behind people's doors," she says, closing the oven door and hugging me, making me cry even harder.

"I won't do it again," I say, resting my cheek on her shoulder.

"Oh yes you will. When I make the transition to the ancestor world, you will be queen and you will definitely do this again—just the right way, Jayd," Mama says, wiping the tears from my face and patting my back. Her warm lavender-scented body comforts me, even though I can feel she's still vexed at me. "There's an order to everything and a reason for that order. Right now you need to concentrate on your studies. You can do things for people within your limitations, Jayd, but only if they ask and you know exactly what you're doing."

"Okay, Mama, I get it now. Trust me, after the day I've had I won't ever go against the rules again."

"Yes, I figured you'd had a bad day from the way Misty charged over here. She asked me what was in the bag you made for her," Mama says, walking into the dining room and picking up the gris-gris from the dining room table, next to the open spirit book. "You need to write down what you put in it and take it to Misty, who's convinced you put some of her hair or blood in it. She's still across the way."

"Are you serious? Do you know what she did to me today?" I say, stepping into the dining room. I was hoping to see a smile on Mama's face, but she's dead serious about this one. "Why do I have to do this?"

"Because you started it, Jayd. Rule number two is to give full disclosure to the client, within reason of course. And asking for the ingredients of a charm made especially for her is within reason. Get to work. I want this settled before dinner."

I can't believe I have to sit here and do more work for Misty after she called me out today. I'm going to be avoiding people for weeks to come over this mess, and now I have to do more work for her. Ain't this some shit?

When I finish recording the ingredients of my "unwebbed" charm bag, I take the list to Mama for approval. After she finished in the kitchen, she went back into her room to rest, I assume.

"Mama," I call through the closed door. "I'm finished with

the list. You want me to check on the cornbread?" I push the door open to see Mama bent down at the shrine, deep in prayer.

"Forgive her, for she knows not what she does," Mama says before she rises from the floor. Her eyes look glazed-over, but they're slowly coming back to awareness.

"Mama, I finished the list," I repeat. Somehow, I don't think she heard me the first time I said it.

"Good. After you take the cornbread out of the oven, go and give the list to your client and come right back. And, whatever you do, don't look Esmeralda in the eyes." She didn't have to tell me that again. I learned my lesson with her powers already. "And Jayd, make sure you taste the bread, you hear?"

"Okay, Mama. I'll be right back." I close the bedroom door and head to the kitchen to take the cornbread out of the oven. She didn't have to tell me to taste it. That's one of the perks of being Mama's helper; taste tests belong to me. After I taste the sweet buttermilk bread I walk through the living room and out the front door to face my wrongdoing, with the charm bag and list in my pocket. If having to serve Misty isn't an ironic punishment, I don't know what is.

"Where are you going?" Jay says as he comes up the drive-way from hanging out at one of his many surrogate homes. "You know you're not supposed to go over there," he says, bending his head toward Esmeralda's house.

"Mama's orders," I say, not wanting to get into detail with him about my mission. I pass him and walk across the small patch of grass dividing our driveway from hers. Most of the houses on our block only have the backyards fenced in, and ours is no exception. I bang my fist on the iron gate, making the birds squawk loudly and the cats wake up from their naps. This house gives me the chills.

"What do you want, witch?" Misty says, coming to the

front door and standing at the gate. She's making this a very difficult task to complete. Why can't she just open the damn gate and let me handle my business?

"Misty, I came to give you this," I say, holding up the bag and paper so she can see it clearly. "Per your request."

"Leave it on the steps and I'll get it when you walk away," she says. At first I think she must be joking, but after I wait a few more seconds for her to open the door, I see she's not. What does she think I'm going to do, hex her on the porch?

"Now you're just being stupid," I say, tossing the items onto the steps, ready to go home and eat dinner. Before I can put the day behind me, Esmeralda and Misty's mom walk out of the house together, both staring me down. My headache returns as I try to focus on Misty's mother, but Esmeralda lures my eyes up with her strong gaze, forcing me to look up at her. Something's helping me look down. I can't explain it, but I feel like my eyes don't belong to me right now and I'm grateful for the assistance.

"What's wrong with you?" Misty says, watching me suffer. "Are you high or something?"

"No," I barely manage to speak. "Esmeralda's got a hold on me and I can't move. I told you I'm not the witch, she is." My headache is getting worse by the minute and I can't yell for Jay or Mama to help me. What the hell do I do now?

"Yeah right, Jayd. Stop being so dramatic and give it up. I know the truth about you and so will the entire school by the time I'm finished." I barely hear Misty's threats as I try to focus on not looking at Esmeralda. Misty's mom stands next to Misty and they both stare at me in disgust, not concerned about my obvious discomfort. How can they be so clueless? I know my face has to show my pain.

"What's wrong with her?" Ms. Truewell finally says, seeing that I'm not going home.

"I don't know. She's always been strange, Mom, you know

that." Esmeralda stays planted at the threshold of her front door, not taking her eyes off me for a second.

"Go back inside, Esmeralda," Mama says, shocking us all. Thank God she came to my rescue. I don't know how long I would have been able to hold off her lethal gaze.

"Your girl crossed the line, Lynn Mae, and you and I both know the rules," Esmeralda says. Misty and her mom both look like they're in way over their heads. "She needs to be taught a lesson in manners and protocol."

"I'll teach her everything she needs to know, don't you worry," Mama says, having the final word. Esmeralda retreats into the house with her faithful clients following right behind her. Free from the painful hold, I turn around and walk slowly back to our yard. I know it's far from over with both Misty and Esmeralda.

"I told you not to do work for people unless they request it," Mama says, vigorously grating the coconut and preparing cocoa butter for my head cleansing. After the episode I just had, Mama immediately prescribed a *rogacion de cabeza* to help rid me of my headache permanently. "There are some things you can't help people out of, Jayd. This is bigger than you or Misty or Misty's mama. Their ill fate goes back for generations and unless they recognize that and want some help to clear it away, there's nothing we can do," she says, mashing the two ingredients together to make a thick paste. "Trying to make potions and charms for people who don't desire change is about as helpful as putting a Band-Aid on a tumor."

"Will her luck get worse because the gris-gris was removed?" I ask, rubbing my temples while I sit on the side of the bathtub, running warm water for my bath.

"It's not Misty's luck you need to be concerned with. You put that energy out there, now it's your responsibility to see it through. If you don't, the bad luck will be yours to deal with, not hers." Mama's job is more serious than I ever knew it to be. No wonder she only takes on a few clients at a time.

"How do I reverse it?" I ask, ready to get this cleansing over with so I can eat dinner. The rest of the family has come home, and there may not be anything left by the time I get done.

"You pray," Mama says, placing the sweet concoction on my head, then moving to my temples and the back of my head. I can feel it already working. "And you need to read up fully on Papa Legba. He can work for or against you, open the crossroads or close them, give you good luck or reverse it. He is the balancing force in nature and must be called upon very respectfully. Otherwise, he'll teach you a lesson you'll never forget."

"So I see," I say. Mama lifts my chin and looks me in the eyes. I see my reflection through her view. She's right; I need to slow it down. It's not my job to save the world and it damn sure isn't my job to save Misty.

"You're a queen in training, Jayd. Don't be in such a hurry to show off your crown. The time will come sooner than you think. Now, remember that as you take your bath this evening. Go on and get started. There are some clean whites in my closet when you finish. And don't worry, I'll set aside a plate for you in my room."

Mama's got a good point. I knew Misty wouldn't be receptive to any kind of help I offered her, but I did it anyway and now I'm the one in need of assistance. Rah's been blowing me up since I got home, and so have my girls. I'll call Rah before I go down for the night. But I don't know what to say to my girls. Maybe they can help me through this madness, because right now I'm feeling the weight of the world on my shoulders and I need some help carrying it. After all, that's what friends are for. And God knows I've helped my girls out of many sticky situations. Now it's my turn to be saved.

~ 15 ~
All in My Head

"I'm a movement by myself/
But I'm a force when we're together."

-FABOLOUS FT. NE-YO

After Wednesday's commotion, I hid out all day yesterday and plan on doing the same thing today. The news of me putting a spell on Misty spread through the main campus as well, giving me no place to hide from people's gawking eyes. I haven't had a chance to catch up with my girls, who seem both concerned and afraid. And truthfully, I still don't know what to say to them. I can't tell them all about my lineage yet. But I'm going to have to give them something.

"Jayd, why are you avoiding us?" Nellie says as she and Mickey approach me outside of my English class.

"Yeah, girl. We've been calling you for the past two days and you haven't returned any of our messages," Mickey says, sporting her new phone for the world to see.

"New gift from your man?" I say, avoiding their inquisition and passing them both up, ready to grab a snack. I didn't spend any time outside yesterday and missed eating my customary Snickers as nutrition. I'll have to make up for that by eating a king-sized one today.

"Yeah, Nigel," she says, caressing the burgundy phone like it's a newborn baby. "He got us matching phones. Now we're in each other's networks."

"Your man didn't have anything to say about that?" I ask, leading the way to the main hall.

"She didn't tell him," Nellie says, wiping the smile right off of Mickey's face. "But for real, Jayd, what's going on with you and Misty? Did you really try to kill her with that bag?"

"If you did, I don't blame you," Mickey says, making us all laugh. I'm glad they're not tripping like I thought they would. "But, real talk though, Jayd. You need to tell us what you're up to."

"Yeah," Nellie says. "I don't need to know everything. Just enough to know what's going on in that little head of yours." She puts her arm around my shoulders. She feels like she's gained some of her weight back from her popularity starvation fast with Tania. I'm glad to have my girls back to normal, or as normal as we can be.

"Yeah, because we didn't know what to say when Misty came up to KJ with that little brown bag, talking about her neighbor saw you bury it behind her door. My first instinct was to call her a lying bitch. But when you verified her story, I didn't know what to think."

"Don't you think if I could've gotten rid of Misty by now that she'd be long gone?" I say, joining the long line of hungry students all waiting to get our midmorning sugar fix.

"You've got a good point," Nellie says, sitting on one of the benches by the snack stand as Mickey joins me in line.

"You don't want anything?" I ask Nellie while Mickey reads the menu.

"No. I'm saving all of my calories for lunch. Chance is taking me to get some Chinese food at the mall. Want to come?"

"I wish I could but I have rehearsal." I miss hanging out with my friends at lunch. Reid and Laura being my new companions doesn't make the time go by any quicker. Chance is lucky he's not in the lead role. He gets a lot more freedom from the stringent rehearsal schedule than I do. But it'll all be worth it when I receive my standing ovation opening night.

"Earth to Jayd," Mickey says. The lady behind the counter looks at me impatiently, as if I've been staring into space for five minutes. "What are you having, girl? You should've let me order first because I'm hungry."

"A king-size Snickers and a bottled water please," I say, sliding my money across the counter in exchange for my treats. Even if I wanted to, I couldn't afford to buy much more than this. Mickey's got two men buying her things and I can't even afford lunch.

"Me too," chimes in Mickey. "And I'll take a bag of Ruffles."

"Damn, Mickey. You keep eating like that and you're going to blow up." Nellie's always so health conscious, but as long as we've known Mickey, she's never gained any weight.

"This one's on me," Nigel says, sneaking up behind Mickey and paying for the both of us. I'm glad they've reconciled for now. It makes things easier for all of us when everyone in our crew is getting along.

"Hey ladies," Chance says as he and Jeremy take a seat next to Nellie. Why is Jeremy still hanging with us when he and I aren't an item anymore? And after Wednesday's drama with Misty, and Rah's possessiveness toward me, I was sure he'd run for the hills.

"How's everything going, Jayd?" Jeremy says, taking a swig of his Arizona Tea. Mickey and Nigel sit on the end of the bench, forcing me to sit next to Jeremy. I'm not ready to talk to him about this, not yet.

"Everything's good," I say. His devious smile lets me know he's not going to let the subject drop. And he has all of next period to bug me to death about it, even if we will be testing.

"Not really," KJ says, walking up to me with his boys right behind him.

"What's your problem?" Jeremy says as he, Chance and

Nigel rise to my defense. I know he's not about to start some more shit with me over Misty.

"My problem is I haven't heard from Misty since Wednesday. What did you do to her this time, Jayd, huh?" he says, lunging at me as Jeremy pushes him back, giving me a rush I didn't expect to feel.

"I don't know anything about Misty and I don't want to. I'm officially out of it," I say, opening my candy bar and taking a bite. I wish I could bite him, but then people would really be talking about me, and my ears are already burning from the gossip circulating.

"Whatever, Jayd," KJ says, allowing his boys to hold him back. Being athletes, they each have something too valuable to lose if they fight. "If I find out you had anything to do with Misty's absences, you'll regret it."

"Did you just threaten her?" Nigel says, stepping forward in full assault mode. Mickey jumps in front of him, blocking his attack. "If you even so much as look in Jayd's direction I'll kick your ass. You hear me KJ?"

"You won't be the only one," Jeremy says, stepping into KJ's face. They are almost the same height, breathing in each other's faces. KJ takes one more look at me before withdrawing his attack and heading back to South Central.

"Thanks, you guys," I say. I can't believe how they all came together for me. Well, all except for Nellie, who stared in amazement at the spontaneous scene. Saved by the bell, we all gather our backpacks and snacks, heading away from the quad and off to class.

"You're going to have to put us on payroll if you're going to need bodyguards now, Lady J," Chance says, giving everyone a much needed laugh.

"I got all of y'all, for real," I say, looking back at my mismatched crew, each with our pictures from the Masquerade Ball dangling from our keychains, Jeremy being the only exception. The only person missing is Rah, who I'll see after school. We weren't able to get together yesterday to make his gris-gris, so I packed the ingredients in my overnight bag, ready to hook him up this weekend.

When Rah picks me up I'm relieved to leave the busy campus. I'm supposed to braid his hair and hang out with our homies, like nothing ever happened. I hope my weekend can stay drama-free. But like most illusions, this fantasy is all in my head too. If I didn't have to face Marty at work, I might have a chance at being peaceful. But I doubt that'll happen.

"Well don't you look cute," Rah says, pulling up to the curb and unlocking the door so I can get in. Mickey, Nigel, Nellie, and Chance are already gone for the day. Rah's running a little behind, but that can be expected in Friday LA traffic.

"You like?" I say, modeling my sleeveless yellow shirt and jeans for him. I even wore my hair down, for a change. I felt like being pretty for myself today. I was tired of hiding. And, other than not following the rules, I didn't do anything wrong and I have nothing to be ashamed of.

"Very much," he says, kissing me as I make myself comfortable in the passenger's seat. "Sorry I'm late, but I had to meet with Kamal's teacher after school. He decided it would be fun to start a water fight at lunch."

"Hey Jayd," Kamal says from the backseat. "I got in trouble at school," he says, sounding as cute as ever. I admire Rah for being such a good big brother. It takes a real man to stand up and take on responsibility, even it means sacrificing life as you know it. Jeremy could learn a thing or two from him.

"I thought I told you to be good when I saw you last weekend," I say, turning around in my seat to see his snaggle-toothed smile shining back at me. "What happened?"

"A girl, that's what," Rah says, making Kamal blush. "He's

got a crush on some little hottie and instead of hollering at her, he decided to spray her with water."

"Sounds familiar," I say, recalling the first time Rah wanted to talk to me in the seventh grade. "You remember what you did, don't you?" I say, making Rah blush too. It's hard to see the rosy cheeks through their dark complexions, but I know they're red with embarrassment.

"No, and neither do you if you want to eat. What do you have a taste for?" he says, pulling off toward Pacific Coast Highway, our usual route home.

"You," I say, slipping my left hand under his right, which is comfortably resting on his thigh. I am in need of an escape and Rah is the only one I want to take with me right now. Rah looks pleased with my choice.

"I want pizza," Kamal says, making my stomach growl.

"Everyone's getting what they want tonight," Rah says, relaxing in his seat as we join the traffic. "We'll order a few extra pies for the session tonight. Do you need to go to your mom's first, or can we go straight to my house?"

"Your house is cool," I say, getting my phone out of my bag to send my mom a text. I wish I could invade her thoughts as easily as she does mine. When I flip my phone open, I see Jeremy has sent me a text.

"I miss you Lady J. We can still hang out as friends. Hit me back soon. J."

"Is everything okay?" Rah says. If he only knew the half of it. I hate to admit that I'm still attracted to Jeremy, but my love for Rah is the real thing and I don't want to mess this up.

"Yeah, everything's fine. I just forgot about something," I say, closing out the message before locating my mom's number in my contact list.

"Don't forget about my charm. Now you got me all hyped

up," he says, sounding like he's about to get a new puppy or something.

"We'll do it when we get to your house. I brought all the stuff with me." I need to be making myself some charms, as much trouble as I keep finding myself in.

"You think so? Imagine what would happen if you'd put all of your talent and energy into helping yourself instead of other people? Why would you waste it on a girl who's proven herself your enemy time and time again?" my mom says in my head. I guess she got my message. *"Yes I did, and it's cool if you don't come straight to my house. Karl's coming over for dinner tonight anyway. Tell Rah I said hi."*

"My mom sends her greetings," I say, folding my phone and putting it back into my purse. Jeremy and I have some unfinished business to deal with and I'm going to have to face it sooner or later. Why is there always baggage in relationships?

"Damn, that was fast. I have to get your service," he says. He can't get with this network unless he's a Williams woman. And no matter how anyone else feels about it, I'm proud to be one of the few.

Today's one of those days I wish I didn't have to be at work. I ended up sleeping over at Rah's house and getting dressed there on the weekends has become second nature. I even have my own towels in his bathroom. It's so nice having a dude around who's not constantly pressuring me to have sex. It makes it easy to be myself around him and he appreciates me the way I am.

"Jayd, can I talk to you for a moment?" Summer says, signaling Sarah to take over the register for the first time since

Marty put her in the kitchen a couple of weeks ago. I know Summer wants to talk to me about my schedule. I already made up my mind that if they don't secure my regular sixteen hours, I'm quitting. What I don't understand is why she waited until the end of the day to deal with this. She and Shahid have been in the office all day, probably picking out matching bathing suits for their upcoming vacation. And I'm not hating on them. I just don't think it's fair that we have to suffer for their happiness. I follow Summer into the office where Shahid and Marty are waiting. Here we go again.

"Have a seat, Jayd," Shahid says in a sour voice. He's never used that tone with me. I wonder what's going on. "Jayd, your register has been consistently short for the past two weekends. The receipts don't match the cash in the drawer. Can you explain this?" Shahid says. Summer takes a seat next to Marty and I feel outnumbered by a pack of wolves. I see there was more than one witch hunt represented in my dream.

"No, I can't. But I'm sure Marty can."

Looking up in surprise, Marty shakes her head and proclaims her innocence. "All I know is that every time I cashed your register out, it came up short." Shahid looks at Summer, and Summer at me. They've already made their decision and I'm losing this battle, plain and simple.

"As long as I've been working here, have I ever given you a reason to not trust me?"

"No, but we can't keep ignoring the pattern," Summer says. Marty smiles at me as she watches me on the hot seat. I don't have time for this mess. I'm done with this place and her conniving ass. I hope Summer and Shahid are happy with a thief as the manager of their restaurant. I hope they see her for who she truly is before it's too late.

"I'm out of here," I say, pulling the black apron over my

head and tossing it onto the desk. "You can mail me my final check."

"Jayd, wait," Shahid says, rising from his seat to come after me. There's nothing left to say. It's five minutes until four. I bet if I walk outside right now Rah will be waiting in the parking lot. "Let's talk about this rationally."

"Shahid, thank you for letting me work here. It's been cool, up until recently," I say, walking across the dining area to clock out for the last time. I'm going to miss my coworkers. I'll have to come and hang out from time to time. I'll also miss the food and the employee discount. But not as much as I miss freedom and respect; two things lacking in this job. "I'll catch y'all later," I say to everyone as I walk out of the front door where Rah is waiting for me, just as I anticipated.

"How was your day?" Rah says, pushing the car door open for me to get in. "You look happier than I've seen you in weeks." Not wanting to spoil my mood, I kiss him on the lips to make him forget about my day, and to help me forget, too. I just want to stay in this moment forever, not worrying about cars or cats or other people.

"It was perfect," I say to Rah as we ride off into the afternoon. The sky is a brilliant orange. I love the early evenings we have in the fall. Ever since the time change last month, it's been getting darker earlier, making for very long nights. And I want to spend most of them getting to know my new relationships with my powers, and with my man.

Epilogue

"It's just like black folks to fire your ass at the end of the day," Jay says, helping me cut up potatoes for our dinner. Mama's at a neighborhood watch meeting and Jay and I are the only ones home. We're making turkey burgers and fries, our favorite meal to co-create.

"They didn't fire me, I quit," I say, slicing the potatoes as he rises from the kitchen table to heat the oil in the cast iron skillet on the stove. "I do agree it was messed up to make me work the entire day. I could've used a Saturday to myself," I say, recalling yesterday's scene. Rah and I hung out all weekend. He even took me out to dinner at Roscoe's Chicken and Waffles, our favorite hang-out back in the day. It feels like old times with him.

"It sounds better when you say fired, like you're a real bad-ass. You should consider altering your story." Jay can be so silly when he wants to. He's more like a brother to me than my cousin, and most of the time I'm glad he's around.

"Jay, you are crazy, you know that," I say, gathering the potatoes in a bowl and passing them to him. Between the two of us, he's the master fryer. My phone vibrating on my hip momentarily distracts me from our conversation. I open it to see Rah's name in the caller ID. I've only been back at

Mama's house for an hour and he's already missing me. This boy is as sprung as he can be.

"Yes, Rah," I say, pretending to be annoyed, but he knows better. "What can I do for you?"

"I wanted to tell you that I've got your back," he says, sounding serious.

"I know you do, baby. And I've got yours too," I say, feeling the need to comfort him. He took it hard yesterday when I told him I lost my job. He's always hated to see me struggle. But we're both hustlers and I'll survive my brief unemployment. I've decided to ask Netta if I could work out of her shop for the time being. I'm even hoping that she'll allow me to build up my own clientele. That's what a sistah really needs.

"What I'm saying is all you need to be doing is braiding hair and doing what you do. And, as your man and your boy, I'm going to see that it happens," he says. If I didn't know better, I'd think Rah could read my mind.

"Okay, now you're scaring me," I say, walking into the living room. I hear another call coming through and see Jeremy's name on the caller ID. What the hell?

"You don't have to be scared with me, girl. I got you, Jayd, and I'm never going to let you down again." As much as I would like to trust him with my heart, Rah has hurt me on more than one occasion. I would love to believe that he can change, but history tells a different story with both him and, more recently, with Jeremy.

I feel a fight coming on. I don't know who it's with or when it's coming. But when it hits, it's going to be a big one and I don't know if I'm ready for it. All I know is that I've got to make some choices, and they start with my happiness and sanity first and foremost. In my world, everything and everyone else is secondary from now on.

Drama High, Volume 5:
LADY J

L. Divine

ABOUT THIS GUIDE

The following questions are intended to
enhance your group's reading of
DRAMA HIGH: LADY J
by L. Divine.

DISCUSSION QUESTIONS

1. Does Jayd have more or less power in her relationships with boys because she hasn't given up the cookies yet? Why or why not?

2. Should Jayd be concerned about Misty, especially to the point of going out of her way to help her? Do you think Misty would do the same for Jayd?

3. Why do you think Jayd is drawn to Misty? Will they ever be real friends again?

4. Do you know of or have a neighbor like Esmeralda? If she were your neighbor, would you be her friend or stay away?

5. Are Nigel and Mickey in love with each other or is it a temporary fling? What's the difference? How can you tell?

6. After everything that went down with Jeremy and Tania, do you think Jayd should give Jeremy another chance? Explain.

7. Was Jayd right to use her powers on Misty without Misty's consent? Was she right to use them to help people in the past without their knowledge? What would you do?

8. Did Mickey's man have a right to be angry with her? If so, do you agree with how he handled the situation?

How would you have reacted as either Mickey or her man?

9. Why does Mama stay with her husband if he's unfaithful? Should she leave him or get another man? Why or why not?

10. Should Lynn Marie be truthful with Karl about her powers? How do you think he'll react?

11. Was Rah righteous in his behavior by being truthful with Jayd about his relationship with Trish? How would you deal with it if you were Jayd?

12. What would be the reaction at school and in her hood if everyone finds out about Jayd's powerful lineage? Should she be straight up about her powers or keep it on the low?

13. Will Jayd's friends be able to handle her destiny or leave her to walk alone? If you were her friend, what would you do?

Stay tuned for the next book in
the DRAMA HIGH series
COURTIN' JAYD.

Until then, satisfy your DRAMA HIGH craving
with the following excerpt from the next
exciting installment.

ENJOY!

Prologue

"*Haven't you heard of no white after Labor Day, Jayd?*" *Mrs. Bennett says, commenting on my bright attire. It's okay for folks to wear all black on any given day. But put on white from head to toe and you stick out like a sore thumb.*

"*Other people's opinions of you don't matter, Jayd. It's what you think of yourself and your heritage that count,*" *Mama says, creeping into my dream as usual. How does she do that?*

"*She's right, Jayd,*" *my mom says. I guess my dream world has become community property. "I know it's difficult sticking out in a crowd, especially at school, but it's worth it. Trust me.*" *And I know she knows what she's talking about. My mom gave up on her spirit lessons in high school. But why are they all up in my head this morning?*

"*Look at that witch,*" *Reid says, no longer in character but joined by the rest of the drama class in his taunting. "My mom told me about people like you.*"

"*Yeah, my great-grandmother remembers hearing stories about slaves with strange powers,*" *Mrs. Bennett says. What is she doing in drama class? She and Mrs. Sinclair don't get along at all. "They had to be put in their place to protect the others on the plantation," she says, raising her pointer above her head, which she yields like a weapon in class on a regular basis, ready to strike.*

"Fight back, Jayd, like I taught you to," Mama whispers into my ear as I stand my ground in the center of the room. Everyone has surrounded me, ready to watch the whipping I'm supposed to receive. "None of our ancestors took shit lying down, Jayd. We come from a long line of warriors. Girl, get up and fight!"

"You have no right to judge me," I say, taking a step back from Mrs. Bennett. None of my friends are here to help me, just the enemies have come to watch. "And you damn sure have no right to hit me," I say. Mrs. Bennett looks at me, her cold blue eyes shimmering like Esmerelda's did when she gave me my headache from hell, which starts again as I stare back at her. What the hell?

Watching me stumble in the center of the circle, the entire class laughs hysterically. I feel like Alice in Wonderland. Any minute I'm going to vomit from the dizziness in my head. The laughing is getting louder and more dramatic. The scene switches, with Reid in character as Macbeth. But instead of being Lady Macbeth, I'm one of the witches. Alia's still laughing, along with the rest of the onlookers, as Mrs. Bennett readies herself to take a cheap shot at me while I'm already down.

"Jayd, don't you hear that alarm, girl? Get up!" Mama yells from her bed, instinctively saving me from my psychic beat-down.

"Sorry Mama. I'm off my game a little this morning," I say, shaking my head free from the pounding left over from my dream. I haven't seen Esmerelda since I gave Misty the list of ingredients I put in her charm bag last week. But I leave out of the back door now always, just in case she's feeling bold one morning. After getting a taste of her powers, I'll never give Esmerelda the chance to catch me off guard again.

"As soon as you realize it's a game that you can master, you won't ever be off of it again," Mama says, giving me insight into my own visions, as usual. How does she do that?

"She's Mama," my mom says, contributing her two cents. "You haven't even seen ten percent of what she can really do. Why do you think I stay out of her way?"

"If your mom's in your head, please tell her to call me. It's time for her to get a reading about this new man of hers," Mama says, rolling over in her bed and returning to sleep. When did I become a mail women?

"Mama says to call her," I say out loud, knowing they both hear me.

"Damn, see what I mean Jayd? She probably already did the reading and wants to see what I have to say. Ain't no hiding from Mama." And don't I know it. I'll have to talk to her about my dream later. Now it's time to get to school and face the music. Things have been really tense since everyone found out about me trying to help Misty and when I came to school wearing all white last week. But I'm not deterred from living my life. And with my crew back together as tight as glue, I know I'll be just fine.

~ 1 ~
Above the Rim

*"The world is mine when I wake up/
I don't need nobody telling me the time."*

—ERYKAH BADU

From my dream this morning I thought my day was going to be much more eventful than it was. It was chill, just going to my classes and getting my assignments for the week. Mrs. Malone still hasn't returned my paper to me. I'm anxious to see what I got on the rewrite. It was a difficult assignment and I wasn't into it at all. I hope there will be a lot fewer red marks across the page when I get it back this time.

I did notice people staring at me, but it wasn't as bad as I thought it was going to be. And me looking extra flyy today gives them a different impression than the one they had of me last week, even though I look flyy in my whites too.

"Jayd, wait up," Nellie says, joining me as I head to the gymnasium. She, Mickey, and the rest of the South Central crew have PE sixth period when I have dance class. But I don't usually see any of them walking because I'm always late for dress up. Hiking from drama class is no joke, and takes the majority of the six minutes we have to pass from one class to the next, no matter how far apart they are. Luckily we have ten minutes to dress, which gives me plenty of time to get ready and be on time for roll call.

"Why aren't you in the gym already?" I say, speed walking

up the steep hill. Students are rushing in every direction before the final bell for sixth period rings. "Don't you have to
run laps if you aren't there for roll call?" Regular PE is different from our elective courses on the AP track, and I always
hear about the different rules from her and Mickey both.
They think I've got it easier because I seemingly have more
options. But, like most books, you can't judge it by its cover.

"Yeah, but we have a sub today," she says, and instantly I
know it's Mr. Adewale, the fine-ass sub who's been working
here for the past couple of weeks. Damn, I wish I had her
class today. "And check it. Nigel, Chance and Jeremy are playing a game of basketball against KJ and his boys. You've got
to come see."

"What the hell are they doing that for?" I say, obviously
more out of the loop than I realized. I missed kicking it with
them at lunch because I was rehearsing in drama class and
nothing seemed unusual at nutrition.

"Because they're boys," Nellie says, pulling me in the direction of the main gymnasium instead of to the back where
the dance studio, Olympic-sized pool, and weight rooms are
housed. I have a good view of the football field from my
class, but the outside basketball courts are on the other side
of the building, which is where all sparring matches are held
unless it's raining, like it's supposed to do this afternoon.

"Yeah, but don't they have football practice now?" Chance
and Jeremy are seniors and elected not to have class last period of the day, especially since they aren't athletes. They'd
usually be at the beach right about now. It's mid-November
and getting cooler, making surfing uncomfortable, I suppose.
But still, a game against KJ is tantamount to suicide and I
can't imagine the fun in that.

"Yeah, but Mr. Donald had a meeting, so the team just has
to run drills and lift weights today. But they all got into it in
fourth period today, arguing about some stupid shit," Nellie

says, shaking her head at the painful memory. "KJ challenged Nigel to a game of one-on-one and Nigel accepted, but it quickly turned into three-on-three when Del and C Money wanted in on the action. Chance had Nigel's back, making Jeremy an honorary team player, of course."

"Of course," I say. I can't believe two of my exes and Rah's best friend are all about to engage in a basketball game. And I wonder what they were arguing about in the first place. "And how did this all start again?" As I step into the gymnasium, the bell rings loudly above our heads. I see Jeremy, Chance, and Nigel on the opposite side of the courts, practicing their free throws. I know Nigel's jump shot is mean. But I've never seen Jeremy or Chance ball.

"I can't remember exactly, but I know it had something to do with money," she says. I hope it isn't about KJ placing bets on me and Jeremy's breakup. Before I can continue my questioning, Mr. Adewale comes out of the boy's locker room in a blue and gray Adidas warm-up suit. Damn, he looks good and he's much taller than I remembered.

"Hey y'all," Mickey says, entering the gymnasium, tardy as usual. "Have they started yet?"

"Not yet," Nellie says, following my eyes across the court. "Jayd, what are you looking at?"

"My future baby-daddy," I say, amusing my girls. I try to make eye contact with Mr. Adewale, but he's got eyes for his clipboard and whistle only.

"I know you're not talking about that nappy-headed teacher, are you?" Nellie's not into natural hair at all. Whenever I wear my hair in Afro-puffs, she clowns me for a week straight. "Jayd, please tell me you don't like dreads."

"What can I say? I prefer a natural black man, especially after dealing with KJ's pretty behind," I say, watching KJ and his boys strut into the gymnasium. Nigel and his team stop and stare down their opponents. KJ and his team face them on the court, ready to ball. They know they've got this game in the bag. I actually feel sorry for my boys. I hope their egos are strong enough to survive the ass-whipping they're about to receive.

"Come on, let's get a seat," Mickey says. As we walk up the bleachers, the rest of my dance class, my dance teacher, and the other sixth-period activity classes file into the open space. I know they're not here to witness the impromptu ball game.

"Jayd, I see you made it to class after all," Ms. Carter says. She's hella cool and basically lets us make up our own routines. I always dance solo so that I can dance to my own music, unlike the white girls in the class who practice their ballet steps all period. I use the class to get a good workout to my reggae and hip-hop CDs.

"Yes, Ms. Carter," I say as my girls take a seat in the bleachers. I hope Ms. Carter doesn't make me go sit with our class.

"Good. I was just about to take Mr. Adewale my roll sheet and didn't want you to get marked absent. The gym teachers have a meeting right now and I'm leaving you to the sub over there. Make sure he knows you're here," she says, leaving me to chill with my girls and flirt with Mr. Adewale. This day's looking up minute by minute.

"I have to check in real quick," I say, tossing my backpack down by my girls' feet and jogging back down the bleachers toward Mr. Adewale.

"But Jayd, you're going to miss the game. They're only playing until the end of the period." Nellie's too into this game for me. I get enough of watching brothas ball from my uncles at home. They have a basketball hoop attached to the top of the garage and ball whenever the mood hits them.

"I'll be right back. Besides, we all know who's going to win." Mickey and Nellie both look at me like I'm the biggest traitor alive. I guess since their boyfriends are playing, it's personal for them. And, I have to admit, I would love to see

Jeremy whip KJ's ass. But I know different. I just hope Jeremy doesn't get humiliated too bad.

"Hello, Miss Jackson," our substitute says as I approach the crowd where my class is standing. My fellow classmates are too busy salivating over him to notice me walk up late. Wait until he's here everyday. Ms. Toni's right, I refuse to be one of these girls. But I do like his style. Maybe for now he can be the big brother I never had. "Glad you could make it this afternoon," he says, giving me a sly smile as he erases the absent mark from my name.

"Sorry I'm late. I was in here the whole time," I say, but I know he's just giving me a hard time.

"It's okay. Have a seat with the rest of the class and we'll begin shortly."

"Oh, but Mr. Adewale," I say, looking across the gym at my girls, who are completely engrossed in the game, and I'm missing crucial moments. "I was hoping I could sit on the other side and watch the basketball game, if it's okay with you." Lord knows I would much rather get to know him better, but I've got to support my boys.

"But your class is over here, Jayd. And your teacher does have a lesson plan here for me to follow, which means I'll need all of the students present. But look on the bright side, you don't have to get dressed today," he says, smiling as he continues to call off names on the roll sheet. How do I get him to cut me some slack? It's not that serious, I know.

"Mr. Adewale," I say, in my sweetest voice. "Can I please be excused, just this one time? It's a very important game and I've already missed the first five minutes." But Mr Adewale isn't budging. Now what?

"Use your eyes, girl. Those pretty brown things are for more than seeing with," my mom says, creeping into my thoughts. But this time, I'm glad. *"Just try it. Keep staring at*

him and think of the outcome you want, like Mama taught
you. And whatever you do, don't let go of your gaze."

"Jayd!" Mickey shouts from across the packed room.
There are a couple of smaller games going on, but most of
the students are kicking it in the bleachers, waiting for the
period to end. "Get your ass over here, girl. We need you."
Following my mother's advice, I lock onto Mr. Adewale and I
can't help but fixate on his flawless butterscotch skin. Looking unmoved at first, Mr. Adewale continues his duties, seemingly unaffected by my plea. But my eyes are wearing him
down and he can't resist my request.

"Fine, Jayd. But make sure you practice your drills at
home. There will be a quiz tomorrow and you will have to
incorporate the drills into your own routine."

"Thank you so much," I say, ready to dart off toward my
girls. "And, can I call you Mr. A?"

"Not if you expect me to answer," he says, smiling at me as
I walk backwards toward my destination.

"Damn, what took you so long? You almost missed the
whole thing." Mickey says, munching on her Funions as Nellie
preps herself in the mirror.

"Don't you think you're exaggerating a bit? And Nellie,
why are you worried about your makeup right now? We're in
the gym."

"So what? The Homecoming princess always represents
the court and I must look flyy at all times," she says, closing
the small compact and returning it to her purse as Mickey
rolls her eyes, trying to ignore our girl. "Besides, Chance will
be devastated after KJ finishes with him and I want to put a
smile on his face."

"Nellie, sometimes you really make my butt itch, you
know that. Homecoming is over," Mickey says, smacking on
the tangy chips. They do smell good.

"You should talk, bringing those stank-ass things in here. You know there's no eating in the gum," Nellie says, pointing to the multiple signs posted throughout the room supporting her claim. "Anyway, I can't believe you're still hungry after that lunch you ate."

"Shut up, Nellie, and watch the game," Mickey says, a little more serious than necessary. I wonder what's got her panties in a bunch?

"Everything okay, Mickey?" I ask, grabbing a Funion out of the near-empty bag. Nellie's right: our girl can eat. "You seem tense today."

"Yes Jayd, I'm fine. I want to watch the rest of the game in peace, if y'all don't mind." No, something's definitely wrong with her. She's being bitchy, even for Mickey.

"Ouch," Nellie says, responding to KJ dunking on Nigel's head. Damn, I know that hurt.

"And that's what we like to call above the rim," Del says, talking shit to Chance as he guards him. "You see all that air KJ left for y'all?"

"Less talking, more ballin'," Jeremy says, stealing the rebound from Cmoney and taking the ball back up the court.

"Oh, so the white boy thinks he can ball," KJ says, but even he can't front: he's impressed with Jeremy's skills. "You're not going to beat me on my own court." Talking shit is KJ's second-best sport. It seems to go hand in hand with being a good basketball player.

"We'll see about that," Nigel says, catching Jeremy's pass and shooting for three. "Did you hear the sound of that? That's what we refer to as a swoosh," Nigel says, laughing all the way back up the court.

"Yeah, well this is what we refer to as a tiebreaker," KJ says, dribbling into Jeremy, through Chance and around Nigel for a perfect lay-up.

"Foul," Chance says, and he's right. But the rules are dif-

ferent in street ball and that's new territory for him and Jeremy.

"Dude, you can't step on someone's feet and still take it to
the hoop," Jeremy says, stepping into KJ's face as the warning bell rings. Most of the students have already started to
head out of the gym to wait for the final bell to ring. My
dance class is still in awe of Mr. A, who's on his way back to
the boy's locker room. And me and my crew are staying posted,
waiting to see if this game will end in bloodshed.

"Dude," KJ says, mocking Jeremy. "There's no referee
here, if you haven't noticed." KJ and Jeremy are the same
height and probably about the same weight. If they fight, it's
going to be an even brawl and I ain't missing a beat, even if I
do miss my bus.

"Yeah, dude. And that's game," Del says, rubbing salt into
their wounds. "Take it like a man."

"I would if you played like one," Nigel says, throwing his
own shit in the mix. "Y'all play worse than the Lakers when
Shaq and Kobe were competing for best bitch of the league."

"Who you calling a bitch?" KJ says, stepping out of Jeremy's face and into Nigel's. Even if Nigel stands a few inches
shorter, KJ doesn't want to mess with him. Nigel was re-
cruited to sack players for South Bay, and he'd be glad to do
it right here on the basketball court, if need be.

"Is everything all right over here?" Mr. Adewale asks, catching us all off guard. Me and my girls are mesmerized by the
scene, waiting to see who will throw the first blow. And Chance,
Nigel, and Jeremy all look ready for the fight.

"Yeah man, everything's cool," Nigel says, being the first to
back down. "This game isn't over."

"Anytime, any place, baby. You call it and I'll be there," KJ
says as he and his team retreat toward the locker room. "It's
going to be my court no matter where we play."

"We'll see about that," Nigel says, passing the ball to

Mr. Adewale as he comes over to give Mickey a kiss before heading back to the weight room. I hope he works off some of that frustration before he hurts someone.

"Jayd, you want a ride? From the looks of it, it's about to storm," Mickey says, suddenly in a generous mood. There must be some magic in Nigel's lips because my girl's mood has completely changed.

"Yeah, thanks. Chance, are you okay?" I say, noticing the black scuff marks across his new kicks—and I know how sensitive dudes can be about their shoes.

"Yeah, I'm cool. Jeremy, you should've kicked his ass when you had the chance, man."

"That's not the way to handle it, trust me," Mr. Adewale says, dribbling the ball and shooting some practice hoops. I see he's got game, too. "But you should have a ref around next time, just in case."

"You're right, man. Next time," Jeremy says, responding to Mr. Adewale but looking at me. I think we should hit the road before I get into some trouble of my own.

"I have to get going," I say, signaling my girls to get up. "Good game. I'm impressed with both of you."

"Why thank you, Lady J," Jeremy says as Chance takes Nellie by the hand, escorting her down the bleachers. "You ladies want to grab something to eat?"

"Oh, I can't. I've got a ton of work to do." I wish I could hang out after school more, like other students do, but Mama would have my ass in a sling if I didn't stick to my regular schedule. "But how about tomorrow? It's an early day."

"Tomorrow it is," Jeremy says, helping me down too. I forgot how much of a gentleman he can be.

"And thanks for being our cheerleaders," Chance says, kissing Nellie's hand as Mickey leads the way out of the gym. I think she's had enough of us and our white boys for one day.

* * *

"Mickey, do you have my sweater in the car?" Nellie says, getting in the back since I'll be dropped off first.

"No. I left it at home. I'll get it to you tomorrow," Mickey says, starting the car as Keisha Cole and Missy Elliot blare out of her speakers, making the trunk shake.

"No, Mickey. I need it now. I have my outfit picked out for tomorrow and it includes my red Bebe sweater. You'll have to take me to your house to get it."

"Ah, hell no. I've got to get home," I say, emphatic about not going to the other side of Compton today. I'm not in the mood for seeing Mickey's family, her man included. "Besides, that's out of her way to go all the way to her house and then back to mine."

"Not if she takes the 105. And besides, you were supposed to give me that sweater back weeks ago. I'm not getting out of this car until I have it in my hand." Nellie can be more demanding than Mickey sometimes. It's a wonder they're friends at all.

"Fine. I'll give you your damned sweater," Mickey says, barely catching the on-ramp to the 105 East from the 110. I don't feel good about this detour in my day at all. I knew I should've taken the bus home, even if it meant getting a little wet. It's better than dealing with Mickey's side of town any day.

START YOUR OWN BOOK CLUB

Courtesy of the DRAMA HIGH series

ABOUT THIS GUIDE

The following is intended to help you get
the Book Club you've always wanted
up and running!
Enjoy!

Start Your Own Book Club

A Book Club is not only a great way to make friends, but it is also a fun and safe environment for you to express your views and opinions on everything from fashion to teen pregnancy. A Teen Book Club can also become a forum or venue to air grievances and plan remedies for problems.

The People

To start, all you need is yourself and at least one other person. There's no criteria for who this person or persons should be other than them having a desire to read and a commitment to discuss things during a certain time frame.

The Rules

Just as in Jayd's life, sometimes even Book Club discussions can be filled with much drama. People tend to disagree with each other, cut each other off when speaking, and take criticism personally. So, there should be some ground rules:

1. Do not attack people for their ideas or opinions.
2. When you disagree with a book club member on a point, disagree respectfully. This means that you do not denigrate other people for their ideas or even their ideas themselves, i.e., no name calling or saying, "That's stupid!" Instead, say, "I can respect your position, however, I feel differently."
3. Back up your opinions with concrete evidence, either from the book in question or life in general.
4. Allow every one a turn to comment.
5. Do not cut a member off when the person is speaking. Respectfully wait your turn.
6. Critique only the idea (and do so responsibly; saying "That's stupid!" is not allowed). Do not criticize the person.

7. Every member must agree to and abide by the ground rules.

Feel free to add any other ground rules you think might be necessary.

The Meeting Place

Once you've decided on members, and agreed to the ground rules, you should decide on a place to meet. This could be the local library, the school library, your favorite restaurant, a bookstore, or a member's home. Remember, though, if you decide to hold your sessions at a member's home, the location should rotate to another member's home for the next session. It's also polite for guests to bring treats when attending a Book Club meeting at a member's home. If you choose to hold your meetings in a public place, always remember to ask the permission of the librarian or store manager. If you decide to hold your meetings in a local bookstore, ask the manager to post a flyer in the window announcing the Book Club to attract more members if you so desire.

Timing is Everything

Teenagers of today are all much busier than teenagers of the past. You're probably thinking, "Between chorus rehearsals, the Drama Club, and oh yeah, my job, when will I ever have time to read another book that doesn't feature Romeo and Juliet!" Well, there's always time, if it's time well-planned and time planned ahead. You and your Book Club can decide to meet as often or as little as is appropriate for your bustling schedules. *Once a month* is a favorite option. *Sleepover Book Club* meetings—if you're open to excluding one gender—is also a favorite option. And in this day of high-tech, savvy teens, *Internet Discussion Groups* are also an appealing option. Just choose what's right for you!

Well, you've got the people, the ground rules, the place, and the time. All you need now is a book!

The Book

Choosing a book is the most fun. LADY J is of course an excellent choice, and since it's a series, you won't soon run out of books to read and discuss. Your Book Club can also have comparative discussions as you compare the first book, THE FIGHT, to the second, SECOND CHANCE, and so on.

But depending upon your reading appetite, you may want to veer outside of the Drama High series. That's okay. There are plenty of options, many of which you will be able to find under the Dafina Books for Young Readers Program in the coming months.

But don't be afraid to mix it up. Nonfiction is just as good as fiction and a fun way to learn about from where we came without just using a history text book. Science fiction and fantasy can be fun, too!

And always, always research the author. You might find the author has a website where you can post your Book Club's questions or comments. The author may even have an e-mail address available so you can correspond directly. Authors might also sit in on your Book Club meetings, either in person, or on the phone, and this can be a fun way to discuss the book as well!

The Discussion

Every good Book Club discussion starts with questions. LADY J, as does every book in the Drama High series, comes with a Reading Group Guide for your convenience, though of course, it's fine to make up your own. Here are some sample questions to get started:

1. What's this book all about anyway?
2. Who are the characters? Do we like them? Do they remind us of real people?
3. Was the story interesting? Were real issues of concern to you examined?
4. Were there details that didn't quite work for you or ring true?
5. Did the author create a believable environment—one that you could visualize?
6. Was the ending satisfying?
7. Would you read another book from this author?

Record Keeper

It's generally a good idea to have someone keep track of the books you read. Often libraries and schools will hold reading drives where you're rewarded for having read a certain number of books in a certain time period. Perhaps a pizza party awaits!

Get Your Teachers and Parents Involved

Teachers and parents love it when kids get together and read. So involve your teachers and parents. Your Book Club may read a particular book whereby it would help to have an adult's perspective as part of the discussion. Teachers may also be able to include what you're doing as a Book Club in the classroom curriculum. That way, books you love to read, such as the Drama High ones, can find a place in your classroom alongside the books you don't love to read so much.

Resources

To find some new favorite writers, check out the following resources. Happy reading!

Young Adult Library Services Association
http://www.ala.org/ala/yalsa/yalsa.htm

Carnegie Library of Pittsburgh
Hip-Hop!
Teen Rap Titles
http://www.carnegielibrary.org/teens/read/booklists/teen rap.html

TeensPoint.org
What Teens Are Reading
http://www.teenspoint.org/reading_matters/book_list.asp?s ort=5&list=274

Teenreads.com
http://www.teenreads.com

Sacramento Public Library
Fantasy Reading for Kids
http://www.saclibrary.org/teens/fantasy.html

Book Divas
http://www.bookdivas.com

Meg Cabot Book Club
http://www.megcabotbookclub.com

DATE DUE

	SEP 10 08
OCT 0 3 2008	
	JAN 0 3 2011
DEC 2 2008	
JAN 0 8 2009	
APR JAN 0 5 2009 2010	
MAY 1 8 2010	
MAY 1 8 2010	
FEB 0 3 2011	

| GAYLORD | PRINTED IN U.S.A. |